WITS & WAGERS

A PRIDE AND PREJUDICE VARIATION

AMY D'ORAZIO

Quills & Quartos
PUBLISHING

Edited by V Lewis, Becky Sun, and Jo Abbott

Cover by Susan Adriani, CloudCat Design

ISBN 978-1-956613-90-2 (ebook) and 978-1-956613-92-6 (paperback)

C olonel Richard Fitzwilliam pushed open the door to his elder brother's bedchamber. Saye's dog, Florizel, growled from his cushion at the side of the room, but Fitzwilliam ignored him in favour of shaking the man-shaped lump beneath the coverlets.

"Go 'way," the lump mumbled.

"I have an idea about how we ought to deal with Darcy."

Saye told him to take his ideas and insert them directly into the place the sun never shone. Fitzwilliam replied by attempting to yank off the coverlets—an unsuccessful manoeuvre, as his brother anticipated him and held on with superhuman strength.

"Leave me alone," Saye ordered, his eyes still squeezed tightly shut. "There is no use. Darcy will propose to Anne and live miserably ever after."

"Anne?"

Saye at last appeared to accept that his wakefulness was required, and so opened his eyes and pushed himself to a seated position. Florizel took this as the signal to leap up beside him. "Our cousin."

"Yes, I know who *Anne* is. He cannot be serious."

"Did you at least bring me coffee?"

"Am I your valet?" Fitzwilliam sank onto the edge of his brother's bed. "Of course I did not bring you coffee."

Saye sighed heavily and rubbed his hands over his face. "I wish you would have. We had the Cognac out last night, and Madeira, and who knows what else, and I assure you that I feel it."

"Took that much to get him talking?"

"Took that much for me to endure it," Saye replied. "He is acting like a schoolgirl about Miss Bennet rejecting him. Too tedious by half. He intends to be in Kent before the week is out."

Fitzwilliam cursed.

"I tried to persuade him to go and court his lady— make another attempt—but he said it was no use. She said something to him like..." Saye paused, seeming to search his memory. "I think something like, if the world was flooded in piss and Darcy lived in a tree, she still would not marry him."

"In those very words, no doubt."

"He says he must surrender to his fate." Reaching beneath his blankets, Saye scratched himself in an area his brother chose not to contemplate.

"But why Anne? He could propose to someone else. I could name you at least ten ladies who would accept him today."

"Because Anne is a certainty. He told me he could

never again risk the rejection he suffered at Miss Bennet's hand. Is she a shrew? Maybe he is better off."

"She is not a shrew," Fitzwilliam replied. "She is, in fact, perfectly delightful."

"Delightful or not, if half of what Darcy told me is true, she can give as good as she gets." Saye scratched again, relating what he could recall of Miss Bennet's choicest remarks by way of Darcy's lovelorn account of events. He concluded with, "I think I might be a bit in love with her myself."

Fitzwilliam heard it all with no little amazement, and replied with a low whistle. "All of that and still he loves her?"

"He says he was angry at first but soon saw the justice of her words." Saye shrugged and began to close his eyes again. "Seems a hopeless business. Perhaps we ought not interfere."

Fitzwilliam leant over and poked him. "Not so hasty. I have an idea. It is rather a drastic one, but I think it is the only hope. How hard did you try to persuade him to go to her?"

"With every power I had in hand. I even offered to pay him. He is a tender little sod—I should hate to see him left to the torment of our cousin and aunt."

"And what did he say to that notion?"

"The details are hazy, of course, but I believe he has decided he is not worthy of her, that he has allowed self-ishness and pride to rule the better part of his character, and that the best thing he can do for her is let her go on to marry another."

"Which is completely untrue," Fitzwilliam replied. "I

must say, Miss Bennet is exceedingly imprudent. Darcy is the second eligible offer of marriage she has refused."

"This is the poor girl we speak of, yes? The one with relations in service and twelve unmarried sisters?"

"Relations in trade and four sisters, but yes."

"So marrying Darcy would be to the advantage of her entire family, even if he did act like a prideful fatwit. Ah, Jones! You darling man!"

The last had been directed at Saye's valet, who had arrived with coffee and the small twists of powders that his master required most mornings.

"Forgive me, Colonel, I did not realise you were here. Shall I fetch you some coffee as well?"

"No, thank you."

Jones bowed and left the room, and Fitzwilliam continued. "If she could be made to reconsider, it would be vastly different for her. Darcy is eager to please her. He tells me he will no longer disdain those around him. He is determined to become a truly amiable gentleman."

Saye took a tentative sip of the coffee. "I would wager anything she does not despise him as much as she thinks she does."

"Why?"

"There are two kinds of hatred—cold and hot. Cold hate comes from indifference, and if she were indifferent, nothing he said would have signified." He took another sip. "She would have shown him the door, and there would have been the end of it. But she fought back."

"Anyone who insults someone's family in such a way is sure to rouse ire."

"Not like that."

"Surely like that," Fitzwilliam insisted.

"If someone you disliked insulted me, or our father, or the earldom, would you have such an argument?" Saye asked. "Or would you tell them to go and hang in chains?"

He had a point. Fitzwilliam never did see the purpose of wasting breath on useless lobcocks. "Depending on what they said of you," he observed with a smirk, "I might well agree."

"That you might," his brother concurred with a chuckle. "In any case, there is nothing you, or I, can do for any of this now—"

"I disagree."

Saye groaned. "I suppose we might make some last attempt to cajole him into—"

Fitzwilliam shook his head. "Darcy will not be easily moved. We have tried consolation, we have tried reason, we have tried persuasion. You have even attempted to pay him."

"What else can be done?"

"Nothing will rouse Darcy so fiercely as defending what is his own, even if what *is* his own is a woman who insists she will *not* be his own."

Saye took a moment and several sips of coffee to understand him. "Ah, another man. Do you know of some other suitor?"

"I know someone who was on friendly terms with the lady who might *appear* to be a suitor with serious intentions."

"Who?"

"Me, idiot."

"You want to marry her too?"

"I do not—but I am not averse to pretending I should like to for a good cause."

Saye yawned. "Darcy will run you through if he discovers you are playing a trick on him."

"Then we shall have to ensure he never finds out."

"And what of the lady? Will she not have her expectations? I am violently opposed to being your second against some country father."

"I have already warned her off," Fitzwilliam informed him. "I told her in Kent that I am too poor to marry cheaply."

"Even so." Saye shook his head. "It will not do for two reasons. One is that Darcy *also* knows you are too poor to marry cheaply. Two, I do not think you are clever enough to play it convincingly."

"I most certainly am. Darcy and I have a lifetime of competing against one another. Do you forget the time we came to blows over a biscuit? I was bleeding in three places by the time he was finished with me."

"And now you will come to blows over Miss Bennet's biscuit." Saye smirked at his own joke. "And when he reminds you that you must marry a woman of good fortune? What will you say to that?"

"A death in the family, and I inherited something."

"Your family is his family," Saye replied reasonably.

"Not on our mother's side. Our mother might have any number of aunts or cousins Darcy knows nothing about."

Saye nodded slowly, the first indication Fitzwilliam had that the scheme might work.

"But I still say you might raise hopes in the lady. If you are persuasive enough for Darcy, then she may believe you have tossed aside practical considerations for her."

"I did think of that," Fitzwilliam admitted, "but there is nothing for it. It will be a fine line to walk, persuading Darcy without raising her hopes, but I believe it can be done."

Saye absently rifled through Florizel's fur while he pondered that.

Fitzwilliam interrupted his musings, knowing just how to raise his brother's interest. "Two hundred pounds says I can make Darcy go to Hertfordshire to woo his lady by pretending that I intend to do the same."

"Two hundred pounds! Faith! You think I care more for Darcy's concerns than I actually do. Fifty pounds if you can successfully provoke him into action."

"Fifty pounds if I get him to Hertfordshire, and another fifty if he proposes again…and one hundred more if she agrees to marry him."

Saye whistled. "You are playing high, soldier, but I shall see you, then. Perhaps we shall find a few others to join in the fun."

"Not too many—Darcy is likely to baulk if he feels himself a source of tattle."

"He will never know about it." Saye finally rose from his bed. "Ring for Jones," he ordered. "We do not have a moment to lose."

CHAPTER ONE

Heartbreak. There was a time—a time not so very long ago—when Fitzwilliam Darcy might have scorned it, deriding it as the stuff of bad novels. But now? Devil take it if the thought of wasting away on a settee, or getting nonsensically drunk, did not appeal to him enormously. From his desk, he glanced longingly at the overstuffed velvet chaise longue near the window. It was a relic from his father's time, and Darcy smiled faintly as he remembered how his mother would recline there, likely with some dreadful novel in hand, while his father sat at this very same desk, writing letters or reading reports from his steward.

Enough of this silliness! He was not some mooncalf. The plans were laid, and soon Miss Elizabeth Bennet would be forgot in favour of nuptial—well, not nuptial bliss. *Nuptial contentment? Nuptial equanimity?* He sighed. Mutual nuptial apathy was the best he could imagine.

The financial rewards of marrying Anne were many.

And Lady Catherine would be happy, possibly Lord Matlock too—certainly happier than either would have been with the announcement that their nephew was marrying a Miss Bennet of Longbourn.

He pressed his hand to his heart and closed his eyes. Would that he could summon the resentment he had first felt after her rejection! It had been so much more enlivening than this despair he presently endured.

The sound of heavy-booted footsteps coming down the hall distracted him from his saturnine reverie. Colonel Fitzwilliam had arrived, appearing to be in high spirits. Darcy straightened himself; his cousins had already heard a great deal about his disappointment and were no doubt tired of the whole affair. No need to show them he was just as dejected as ever.

"There you are." Fitzwilliam settled comfortably into one of the chairs across from Darcy's desk. "Thought I might see you at Boodle's."

Darcy rose and went around his desk to sit in the chair beside his cousin's. "Why? Something happening there?"

"Card game. Reportedly, they have been there all night, and the stakes are grown rather dear. Pinkerton is likely to lose the very shirt off his back."

Darcy shook his head and offered a drink, which his cousin refused.

"I cannot stay long, Darcy, but I have some news that I simply could not wait to acquaint you with. And if you should feel inclined to offer any advice, or help along the way"—he tipped an imaginary cap—"I should be much obliged."

"Anything I can do, of course. What is it?"

"You will recall my mother's aunt, Lady Peyton?"

"Um...no. I cannot say I do." Darcy crossed his legs and made himself more comfortable. Fitzwilliam, it seemed, was in the mood for an epic telling of his tale.

"She was the widow of Sir Henry Peyton of Salt Hill in Middlesex. I cannot even tell you how old she was, but the rumours say that she danced with the first King George at her coming out."

"Positively ancient, then."

"In February, she died," Fitzwilliam continued. He had apparently decided to accept that drink after all, but being a frequent *habitué* of the house, he retrieved it himself. "She died in full control of her faculties, fortune, and estate—and childless."

"A wealthy, childless aunt?" Darcy raised his eyebrows. "No doubt an untold quantity of previously unknown heirs have presented themselves?"

"No entail," Fitzwilliam said, returning to his chair and swirling his drink around. "The lady could dispose of the property according to her own pleasures, and it seems my mother was the last person on earth who truly cared for the old dear. Visited her regularly and assisted where she could, which none of Mother's other cousins ever did."

"Dare I imagine that she is to be rewarded handsomely for this kindness?"

"Yes, she is. My mother is to receive Lady Peyton's estate. The fortune is to be divided, but the house and lands are now under the control of Matlock."

"Excellent news!" Darcy exclaimed.

Fitzwilliam raised one hand to stay him, still beaming happily. "I have not got to the truly excellent part yet."

"Which is?"

Fitzwilliam's eyes twinkled above a broad smile. "She is giving it to me."

"The house?"

"The house, the land—all of it."

Pleasure ignited in Darcy's chest. His cousin's prospects had long weighed on him, particularly as Fitzwilliam had seemed increasingly intent on throwing himself in the line of French fire. Now, hopefully, he would stay in England, tend to his house, perhaps even marry. A smile, his first true smile in weeks, spread across Darcy's face. Unable to speak, he merely reached across the divide between them and clapped his cousin's shoulder.

Rising from his chair, Darcy went to the sideboard to fill his own glass. He brought the decanter back and added more to the small portion his cousin had served himself. "We must toast your change of fortune."

"Very well, but not too much. Saye tells me he will begin instructing me on the ways of estate management—"

"Saye? What does he know?"

"Nothing at all. But I must permit him to think himself the wise elder brother in case I ever *do* require his assistance."

"Wise indeed." Darcy raised his glass. "To land ownership! May your fields drain nicely, your crops flourish, and a lady of the house be found forthwith!"

Fitzwilliam drained his glass, chuckling at the last.

"Ah yes, a lady of the house. Scarcely were the words 'I am giving you Salt Hill' away from my mother's lips before she began urging me to take a wife."

Darcy grinned. Lady Matlock's desire to see both of her sons settled was not hidden. "I am sure you have any number of lovely young possibilities now. Miss Roberts seemed rather taken with you at the party at Warwick House."

"A charming girl, but too young by half. I think she is just seventeen, and I should prefer a wife not counted among the ranks of Georgiana's friends."

"They do seem to get younger, do they not? What of Lady Phyllida Holmes? She is two and twenty, and as clever as she is pretty."

"Mm," said Fitzwilliam dismissively. "I confess my eye has been drawn to another. I believed she was out of reach, but now…"

"Lady Harriet Thorpe?"

He shook his head. "No, not Lady Harriet, but the lady does have similar dark hair and eyes."

The first niggling of a suspicion entered Darcy's mind but was summarily dismissed. "Who is she?"

"Miss Elizabeth Bennet."

Darcy congratulated himself on the fact that, although it felt as if lightning had struck him, he did not respond as violently as he might have wished to. An ill-timed sip made him cough and sputter, but that was all. Removing his handkerchief from his breast pocket, he dabbed at his lips, allowing time for the recovery of his composure. Nevertheless, his voice sounded strained and anxious when he said, "Surely not?"

"I know what you are thinking." Fitzwilliam held his hands up to ward off Darcy's protest. "How could I wish to marry a woman who had spoken so cruelly to my own cousin? But I think with time, the two of you could easily lay down your arms."

Darcy wondered whether he had fallen asleep and was dreaming. Was there some demon on his chest, the *mara* of old Norse mythology, causing these dreadful notions to be spewed at him? "Lay down our arms! H-how can you even consider—"

"I know, I know! There are other considerations, such as your own strictures against the lady. I have considered them, I assure you. The undistinguished family. No fortune of her own. Not a prudent match in any way altogether. But Darcy, I *like* her, and given the removal of my prior limitations, I daresay I could be in a fair way towards falling in love with her."

Had Fitzwilliam gone mad? Yes, they had always competed against one another for *things*. Two men close in age, raised as brothers, would either be dearest friends or famous enemies; he and Fitzwilliam had taken their turns at both. But this was not some contest to see who could throw a rock the farthest, or anything so inconsequential. This was the woman he *loved*.

Feebly, not even knowing what he was saying, he blurted, "But...but she is...she has gone back to Longbourn. Hertfordshire. Her family, they do not come to town." As if *that* was the greatest objection to this!

"It does present some difficulty, to be sure," Fitzwilliam said agreeably. "That is why I hoped perhaps you might be a fine fellow and arrange something with

Bingley at his place there. We shall go and rusticate on some flimsy excuse of fishing or shooting or such, and see what transpires. What say you?"

An image sprang to mind of Fitzwilliam strolling in the maze at Netherfield with Elizabeth smiling and laughing on his arm. A roaring sound filled Darcy's ears and his head swam, and before he knew what he was doing, he shouted, "No. No!" He set his glass down, wincing at the bang it made; he had not intended to do that. "You cannot...Elizabeth... No! You will *not* do this."

Fitzwilliam startled when Darcy's glass slammed onto the desk. He stared, first at the glass and then at his cousin before saying, with infuriating calm, "Darcy, I knew you might not be wholly pleased by this, but pray consider my interests above your own for once."

"It is not selfishness that—"

"What else could it be? You are off to Kent to propose to Anne, are you not? I say Miss Bennet is fair game."

Panic thrust Darcy upwards out of his seat. "Fair game? How dare you speak of her so?"

"What do you call it then? You would not wish her to remain unmarried forever. Is that to be her punishment for refusing you, that no man could ever have her?"

Another man. It was not the first time Darcy had imagined her in the arms of another, but it *was* the first that he had imagined her in Fitzwilliam's arms. Darcy leant against his vacated chair for several long moments, willing his gorge to settle, then walked towards the window, staring down at the street below.

Behind him, Fitzwilliam said, "I should hope you would wish us both well."

"I shall not." Darcy turned to his cousin and thrust a pointing finger in his direction. "She is not for you, and *that* is the material point."

"Who says? You?" Fitzwilliam challenged him, arms crossed over his chest.

Darcy took a deep breath. "She is not a suitable wife for either of us, if you care to examine it with a clear head. She is cousin to Lady Catherine's parson!"

"Who, himself, will be a landowner one day," Fitzwilliam observed.

"When her father dies."

"Yes, Darcy, that is how most of us inherit land... because someone died. You included."

"H-her family...her mother! You could never see her mother and yours in a room together."

Fitzwilliam shrugged. "Then I shall not *put* them in a room together. I do not wish to marry her family."

"She is...she is uneducated. They never had a governess, she and her four sisters."

"Neither did I."

"You did!"

Fitzwilliam shook his head slowly. "Saye put frogs in her bed and ran her off and got himself sent away to school. He liked it so well, his lordship followed suit with me, as did your father with you two years following."

"I had a governess until I was nine," Darcy retorted. "At Pemberley."

"Well done, you," Fitzwilliam replied sarcastically. "Nevertheless, I did not, and nothing you say will convince me I did. And what does it signify? Miss Bennet is clever and sweet, and I do not care two straws how she came to be that way."

"She lacks...she lacks the birth, the...the...town bronze, if you will. You have seen all her finest gowns, you know! The ladies in town would never accept her as one of their own."

"Darcy." Fitzwilliam shook his head. "I admit I had some reservations about coming to you with this, but everything you have just said verily proves what I believe."

"Which is what, precisely?"

"That you *think* you love her more than you actually do."

It was such a shocking thing to say that Darcy laughed. "What?"

"I think what you are really upset about is the injustice of it all. How dare she refuse the great Fitzwilliam Darcy something he wants!"

Never before had Darcy so wished to punch his cousin right in his smug face, but he restrained himself. "You are wrong."

"Am I? You met her when? Last autumn?"

Darcy did not reply.

"If my memory serves me, it was October, nine months or so ago, at an assembly during which you refused to stand up with her and insulted her in front of her friends and relations."

"I told you why I—"

"And you certainly have never had any good to speak of her since then. Even in this conversation, you have only disparaged her and insulted her family. Not much the look of love, from my angle."

"My reservations with regard to her connexions and upbringing—"

"Have been detailed at length," Fitzwilliam replied with a roll of his eyes. "Your inclination for the lady was rather easily conquered by your pretensions. Forgive me but that, sir, is not love."

Darcy restrained his fist, but he did hurl a few curse words at his cousin.

Fitzwilliam chuckled. "Speak as you like, Darcy, but to all of that I shall add that when presented with a challenge, your response was to curl up in your den for a few weeks and then run off to marry your cousin. I am afraid you have a very sorry idea of love."

"It was a scathing, painful rejection—not merely a challenge!"

"Either way," Fitzwilliam continued, "it is done. You have said yourself that any future intercourse is impossible, so I thought, 'Why not?'"

"Fie on that!" Darcy interrupted angrily. "Not impossible, not at all. Pursue her if you wish, but you will need to go through me."

"What?" Fitzwilliam stared at him in an exaggeratedly disbelieving way. "You told Saye yesterday that you were on your way to Kent to propose to Anne, and now—"

"I have had a change in plans," Darcy retorted tightly. "I intend to win Miss Bennet instead."

"You would not stoop to paying court to her simply to outdo me?"

"I shall outdo you, because I love her and you do not, and thus do not deserve her."

"I am certain I could make Miss Bennet fall in love with me ten times over before she would grant you the slightest measure of her affection, Darcy. Indeed, she might be in love with me already, for it was I, and only I, who dedicated myself to her amusement at Rosings."

"You did, that is true. I think it very likely she considers you a fine *friend*."

Fitzwilliam crossed his arms over his chest. "She will not think of me merely as a friend for long, not once I set my mind to it. Do recall, in matters of courtship, I am far and above your master. I spend most of my time warning women *against* falling in love with me."

Darcy returned to his chair. "You think far too much of yourself."

"It does a man good to know poverty and hardship. I have been required to develop other means by which I might draw the attention of the fairer sex. Forgive my boasting, but in such arts, I am unequalled."

"Certainly at Rosings you were unequalled. I doubt there is another bachelor under the age of sixty in the whole county," Darcy countered drily.

"Save for *you*," said Fitzwilliam. "And yet she spent her time with *me*."

Darcy felt his gut tighten, but he spoke evenly when he said, "I know how to win a lady's heart as well as the next man does."

"I have never seen it."

"Just because you have not seen it does not mean I am incapable of it."

"What I have seen is your habit of keeping the ladies at a distance. Old habits die hard, do they not?"

"I love Elizabeth Bennet, and I shall do whatever it takes to win her, against any man, be he relation, friend, or foe. You may depend upon it."

Fitzwilliam stood. He wore no sword, so it was a second or two before Darcy understood his upright stance and his meaning in raising his right arm, palm straight and pointed left, over his face, then lowering it sharply. A fencer's salute.

Darcy rolled his eyes but then returned the gesture. "You pledge me a fair fight then?" he asked wryly.

"With all honour," Fitzwilliam replied.

There was a silence between them as Darcy—and his cousin too, he supposed—considered the words that had passed between them. Fitzwilliam was first to drop his gaze, though there was no shame in his countenance. He looked, to Darcy's eye, quite pleased with himself.

At length, Darcy said, "Let us begin by going to Bingley. If we have no means to so much as *see* the lady, this entire contest becomes near to impossible."

CHAPTER TWO

The two gentlemen exited Darcy's town house in silence. Darcy's carriage had been brought round, and Fitzwilliam stopped briefly to look at it.

"Something wrong with my carriage?" Darcy asked as they entered and settled themselves.

"Did you not tell me you had lately commissioned one new?"

"I did."

"An engagement present for Miss Bennet, was it?" Fitzwilliam regarded him with an impertinent grin and raised brows.

"A premature commission, but yes," Darcy replied, feeling a flush of embarrassment heat his face. He hoped the shadows within the carriage concealed it. He reached up to knock, signalling his men to begin driving.

Fitzwilliam shook his head. "If you had spent more time considering the proposal itself, and less time commissioning engagement gifts, we would not be having this conversation."

Darcy did not reply to that.

"I daresay it was an appropriate gift for her, though. From what you have said, I should imagine Miss Bennet does not have her own conveyance."

"The Bennets had one carriage that I ever saw. I know not if there were others."

"Then perhaps we ought to sweeten this wager a bit," Fitzwilliam suggested. "If you lose, the carriage is mine to give to her."

"And if you lose? What shall I have?"

"I do not intend to lose," Fitzwilliam replied loftily. "Like I always tell my men—if you go into battle imagining defeat, then you are sure to be defeated. The vision of victory must always be in mind."

Darcy clenched his jaw and looked out of the window. Fitzwilliam was behaving like a presumptuous idiot, but that hardly signified. An uncomfortable truth was beginning to take root within him: Fitzwilliam might win. Elizabeth liked his cousin, and she hated him. The advantage was his cousin's.

You wish me to keep victory at the forefront of my mind, and so I shall.

~

At their club, they found Bingley seated at a table full of younger gentlemen. His appearance—cravat wilted, hair tousled, eyes red-rimmed—led Darcy to believe that they had all been at the infamous game at Boodle's, likely all night.

He and Fitzwilliam took their seats and sat for a time, mostly in silence among the chatter. They were not gentlemen Darcy typically consorted with, nor did his cousin. They were a younger set, men whose money was new and for whom London life remained nothing but an endless round of parties. Nevertheless, uninterested as Darcy was in the discussion, he found his ears pricking up at several references to Bingley's 'angel' and the general understanding that there would be, soon, one less man among their ranks.

When at last the others had excused themselves, Bingley offered a smile to his friend. "Darcy! Colonel! Have you heard about this nonsense they got up to at Boodle's?"

"A little." Fitzwilliam signalled to the servant to bring fresh drinks. "Forgive me, we did not intend to send your group scurrying off."

"No matter. We were ready to call it a day. The balls will likely be devoid of men tonight." Bingley chuckled. "Everyone is either too tired, or too determined to settle scores, to dance."

"Have they finished? What was the worst of it?" Fitzwilliam asked.

"When I left, Mr Stephen Fox was down nearly five thousand," Bingley reported. "I believe that was the worst of it, though there were so many side bets going on, one can only guess."

"People betting on other people's hands?" Darcy asked.

"Betting on others' hands, betting on how much would be lost or won, betting on how many times a man might relieve himself." Bingley laughed. "It was madness, utter madness."

"Sounds…deplorable," Darcy managed.

"All in good fun. How was Kent? You were both there, I think?"

"We were," Fitzwilliam answered. "Quite an agreeable visit, if I do say so."

"Nothing like the country when the weather gets warmer," Darcy added.

"That is true," Bingley owned. "But London is charming at this time of year as well."

"I understand your country place is rather nice," Fitzwilliam said. "Hertfordshire, is it not?"

"Oh, I only leased Netherfield Park," Bingley told him. "And as it happens, I have given it up."

"Given it up?" Darcy exclaimed. "Why did you do that?"

Bingley did not look at him as he explained, "An eligible purchase offer was made for it. The Suttons of Devon have purchased it for a second son, I believe."

"Hugh Sutton?" Fitzwilliam shot Darcy a look. "Good-looking fellow, well seated."

"He is a dandy," Darcy said with a reproving sniff. "I am shocked he found the place fashionable enough for him."

"A few hours on a horse gets him to Bond Street," Fitzwilliam replied. "It will do."

"I heard he is lately engaged," Bingley said. "No doubt he needed a place to take his bride."

That much was a relief at least. Darcy need not add Hugh Sutton to his list of competitors.

"It sounded like a rather agreeable county. We had intended to beg an invitation from you," Fitzwilliam said with his usual bonhomie.

"Would that I could offer one," Bingley exclaimed warmly. "As it stands, I shall only be there again...um, briefly."

As Bingley said so, he appeared to take great interest in the tankard he had only just emptied of ale. He picked it up and attempted to drink; then, finding it empty, he set it back on the table and stared into it for a few minutes before he suddenly said, "Well, Darcy, this might be the last time you speak to me."

Darcy exchanged a glance with his cousin. "Why would it be the last time I speak to you?"

Bingley crossed his arms over his chest. "I am getting married."

"Married?" Darcy exclaimed. His cousin began to proclaim his delight and well wishes. A fraction of a second too late—and not missing the look Bingley sent him—Darcy joined in the felicitations. "May I ask who the fortunate young lady is?"

Bingley sighed. He fidgeted and shifted, then sighed again. At length he said, "Hang it all. I know you will not approve, but as Shakespeare said, 'To your own person be truth.' Or is it 'Mine self be the truth?' 'Speaketh mine own truth?' Whatever it is—you know I do not have a head for such things!"

He paused, and Darcy prodded gently, "The lady's name is...?"

"Jane Bennet." Bingley met his gaze squarely. "I am going to marry Miss Jane Bennet."

Darcy winced, not meaning to. He should have gone to Bingley and told him what he had learnt from Elizabeth—that Miss Bennet did love him. He had not considered it because he was too enmeshed in his own misery to even think of Bingley. *Selfish disdain for the feelings of others* echoed uncomfortably through his mind.

He recognised, suddenly, that his wince might have been perceived differently and so offered Bingley a smile, trying to seem placating. "I am happy for you, Bingley. Truly, I am."

His friend seemed to sag with relief. "Do not think that I easily disregarded the counsel you and my sisters so kindly offered. I could not, and I would not. But then I realised something I had not before considered."

"What was that?" Darcy asked.

"None of you—not you, not Caroline, not Louisa—could have known or comprehended any of my more private meetings with Miss Bennet, the conversations between the two of us, or the things of that nature. You believed her heart was not easily touched—"

"I did, that is true, but I do recog—"

"I think she merely had a lady's proper reserve—perhaps more than most, I shall grant you that." Bingley raised his empty tankard to his lips again, then set it down, signalling to the manservant to bring another. "Only I knew what had passed between us, the words that were said, the quiet looks...things which to me indicated that she did hold me dear. None of you knew anything of those."

"That is true," Fitzwilliam interjected, and Darcy gave him a black look.

"But you thought her indifferent to me, and I thought she loved me. The only way to know the truth of it, I reckoned, was to go and see her. So I went back to Hertfordshire. I needed to meet with Morris again about Netherfield, so it was not a wasted trip—only I arrived to find she was right here in London! Has been since after Christmas."

Bingley fixed his eyes on Darcy, his gaze level as he said, "But I think you knew that."

The manservant came then, bearing fresh tankards of ale. While he placed them on the table and gathered up the emptied ones, Bingley's gaze did not falter, and Darcy resisted the urge to squirm beneath his friend's cool blue stare.

The servant gone, he admitted, "I did know it, and I have nothing to say for it but that I pray you will one day forgive my unpardonable interference in the matter. It was badly done."

"It was," Bingley acknowledged. Then, with a dizzying shift towards geniality, he smiled broadly. "But I can offer my forgiveness if you will offer me your blessing."

Relieved, Darcy mirrored his smile. "You do not need my blessing, but if you want it, then of course you shall have it. I am happy for you, and wish you and the future Mrs Bingley every happiness."

Fitzwilliam offered his own good wishes, and both men shook Bingley's hand in turn. There were, then, some minutes spent in rhapsodising about Jane Bennet, the love affair between them, and the like.

"Knowing you are engaged to a daughter of the county, I am surprised you did not wish to purchase Netherfield yourself," Darcy said when it was done.

"Are you?" Bingley took a long draught of ale and quirked a brow. "Given your opinion of my future family, I should think it perfectly obvious why I want to give the place up. Even Lizzy has said that a lady might be settled *too* near her family."

Bingley laughed even as Darcy felt his heart leap at the mention of her. He bowed his head, conscious suddenly of Fitzwilliam's gaze upon him.

"But it was Jane who did not have a mind to settle there," his friend continued. "Who was I to argue?"

"Indeed," Fitzwilliam replied warmly. "Hardly seems a right way to begin. If the lady wishes to be gone from the neighbourhood, then I say be gone."

Darcy shot his cousin another look intended to be quelling, then said, "Bingley, I truly am very pleased for you. Pray do not doubt it for an instant. I do not have any ill feeling towards your future relations."

"Thank you."

"Where will you live, then? Much as I dislike to meddle in your affairs—"

Bingley raised his brows, which Darcy acknowledged with a rueful grin.

"That is to say, meddle *further* in your affairs. I do know of a situation near Pemberley. Splendid land, lovely parks, although it must be said that the house itself is in woeful need of modernising. Unless Miss Bennet prefers the fashions of the Stuart era?"

Bingley laughed. "I should think not! Thank you. Perhaps I can persuade her to go and see the place."

"Do you plan for a long engagement?" Fitzwilliam asked.

"My wedding is scarcely a month from now," Bingley announced, naming a date in the middle of June.

"So soon?" Darcy asked.

"Soon? Being that I have loved her since the first day I saw her, these nuptials feel insufferably delayed."

"No, no, I only meant that…" Darcy shook his head. He was surprised, that was all. "I wish you well, Bingley."

"Well enough to…" Bingley stopped, shaking his head. "No. I cannot ask it of you."

"You can," said Fitzwilliam, eagerly inserting himself into the conversation. "You will do anything, will you not, Darcy?"

"Bingley, whatever you need done will be my greatest honour to do."

"Even if I ask you to stand up with me?" Bingley asked. "I know how much you disliked being there, and I hate to ask it of you."

"I should be honoured," Darcy repeated firmly. "Truly."

"The neighbourhood has planned a great many events," Bingley explained, his face turning a dull red. "It is not merely the breakfast, but of course you need not accept any invitations you do not like."

"What else could there be?" Darcy asked, causing Bingley to flush more deeply red.

"Whatever it is," Fitzwilliam hastened to intrude, "I am sure it will all be done in good taste."

"I shall be glad to partake in whatever festivities are planned," Darcy said.

Bingley's unease appeared to dissipate. "Mrs Bennet thought it a right thing that I should celebrate with a ball at Netherfield—as a compliment to my bride. I set Caroline to planning that."

"Mrs Bennet sounds very wise," Fitzwilliam offered.

Darcy resisted the urge to roll his eyes. "I am sure the future Mrs Bingley will be pleased to have you fete her amid her family and friends."

"That is to be two days before the wedding itself. There will be an assembly, a dinner at Longbourn, as well as a party at Lucas Lodge…a card party at the Robinsons'—"

"I do not think I am acquainted with any Robinsons," Darcy said.

"You met Mr Robinson on several occasions last autumn. He is rather a quiet fellow, I suppose. He is married to Mr Bennet's cousin and lives at Gorham House. They have a son at Cambridge—I am sure he must have mentioned it to you."

Darcy opened his mouth, intending to speak, and then closed it again. Insisting that he did not know Mr Robinson could only emphasise the fact that he had not bothered to remember some of the principal families of the neighbourhood wherein he had stayed for two months.

An unsocial, taciturn disposition, unwilling to speak...

Elizabeth's words leapt into his mind. How disagreeable, how above his company he had behaved! Was it any wonder she had disliked him so? To not even trouble himself to know her cousin?

Fitzwilliam was once again quick to insert himself, no doubt eager to show himself the more genial cousin. "I am sure it will be a pleasure to be acquainted—or, in Darcy's case, re-acquainted—with Mr Robinson and his family."

It was a strange thing to say for a man who was not, as yet, included in the invitation; indeed, a man who had no reasonable cause to be at Bingley's wedding. But as was his custom, Bingley betrayed no offence at the presumption. He grinned at Fitzwilliam and mentioned the multitudes of pretty girls he might come to know in Hertfordshire, urging him to come to Netherfield as soon as he could.

And just like that, the game was on.

CHAPTER THREE

"I fear I may have caused us a wrinkle."

Fitzwilliam had presented himself in Darcy's dressing room, having arrived at the house at an early hour the next morning. He leant against the door frame, giving his cousin a piercing look.

"What wrinkle?" Darcy enquired as he donned the waistcoat his man handed him and buttoned it. He had lost weight, it seemed, for it did not fit as snugly as usual.

"This wager of ours. I made the mistake of telling my brother about it."

"Wager?" Darcy asked. "The carriage, you mean?"

"Oh, no, I misspoke. Not a wager as much as a…well, never mind what we call it—that both you and I wish to woo the same lady." Fitzwilliam appeared at ease, though to Darcy it seemed his words were glib.

Suitably attired, Darcy dismissed his man and turned to fully face his cousin. "Regardless, surely we may count on his discretion?"

"When can we ever count on Saye for discretion?"

Darcy heaved a sigh of disgust as they exited his dressing room and walked towards the front stair. "As he does not know her, nor anyone connected to her—"

Fitzwilliam shook his head. "No, but he will himself be connected to her once he is her brother."

"Saye will undoubtedly delight in a nearer connexion to Bingley," Darcy replied sarcastically. Saye's dislike of Bingley's puppyish enthusiasm was well-known to both of them. "How do your mother and father like it? Have you told them of your scheme?"

They had arrived in the vestibule, and Darcy mentioned the possibility of looking in at their club. As such a scheme was agreeable to his cousin, they both departed.

"Naturally my family had their own plans and wishes for who would be my wife," Fitzwilliam acknowledged. "Ladies whose families would bring some political advantage or who had a sizeable fortune to bring to the marriage. But I told them straightaway that none of the ladies they liked would suit me. Fortunately, they still have Saye's marriage to preoccupy them."

"Saye's marriage?"

"Should he ever happen upon a woman who can tolerate him for longer than a dance."

The club was relatively empty, given the early hour. Darcy would not have expected Saye to be present—his eldest cousin often said that nothing of importance ever happened before two in the afternoon—but there he was, seated at a prominent table.

"The Great Master of Pemberley," Saye intoned theatrically as they approached him. "Locked in a battle of the heart against the second son of the Earl of Matlock. Will it be tall, handsome, and scandalously wealthy who prevails, or fat-witted but amiable?"

Fitzwilliam chuckled and gave his brother a little shove before sitting.

"What is that scent you are wearing?" Saye enquired of Darcy as he took a seat opposite him.

"Do you dislike it?"

Saye was busily wafting the air between them towards his nose. Wrinkling his brow, he said, "Oakmoss, to be sure...the faintest touch of amber, perhaps a cinnamon top note? Who blends this for you?"

"It is derived from Houbigant's creations."

"Is it new?"

Darcy sighed heavily. "What does it matter?"

"I think you ought to be differently scented when you next meet your lady. You do not wish the smell of rejection to be yet lingering."

"A valid point, though I should prefer that you not bandy it about so loudly here in the middle of our club," Darcy replied glumly. "That said, it does remind me of a request I have for you."

"Of course."

Saye was on intimate terms with a notorious smuggler called Gertie Birdsell. For exorbitant prices, Gertie ensured that Saye had as much champagne, brandy, tobacco, lace, and fine-milled French soap as he desired. The entire family was aghast that Saye did business with such a criminal, but that only made Saye like Gertie more.

Darcy positively loathed being involved in any such

doings, but it had occurred to him that gifts for some of the ladies of Meryton—those who had hosted him, fed him in their homes—might raise the public opinion of him. And if that opinion happened to work its way back to Elizabeth…even better. Without looking at his cousin, Darcy described what he wished for and in what quantities.

"Easy enough," Saye replied. "Twenty pounds should do it, but give me an extra ten just in case."

"Thirty pounds!" Darcy exclaimed. "Have you taken leave of your senses?"

"Fine French goods do not come cheaply, and one must account for the risk to life and limb poor Gertie must face daily. You know he is Prinny's cousin?"

"No, he is not," Darcy replied flatly. Gertie's lineage grew more exalted every time Saye spoke of it.

"He absolutely is, and I can prove it unequivocally."

"I am not certain such libertine connexions can be to his credit, in truth, but I do not really care. I shall send Fields over later with the sum. Just arrange it for me," Darcy replied sharply.

"What on earth do you need so much soap for?" Fitzwilliam asked.

"Gifts."

"Greasing up the mothers, are you?" Saye nodded approvingly. "Well done, my boy. I am going to bet you a hundred pounds that you will win Miss Elizabeth Bennet." He extended his hand towards his cousin to shake on it.

"You want me to bet against myself?"

"Well, who do *you* think will get her?"

Darcy frowned, but before he could say anything, there was Mr Alfred Hurst poking his nose in. "What's the game, men?"

"Nothing," Darcy hastened to say. "No game."

"Darcy and Fitzwilliam both want the same woman," Saye informed him. "Darcy will not bet, but perhaps you will?"

Hurst's eyes lit up, and he rubbed his hands together with glee. Uninvited, he sat, putting his chin in hand to peer at both Darcy and Fitzwilliam carefully. "And the lady is...?"

"Miss Elizabeth Bennet," Fitzwilliam said helpfully.

Darcy barely stopped himself from kicking him.

"Which one was that?" Hurst asked. Then, with a charmless waggle of his brow and a gesture towards his chest, he asked, "The, um, well-padded one, no doubt?"

"The one who stayed for above a week at Netherfield to nurse Miss Bennet," Darcy informed him with an annoyed sigh.

Hurst's brow wrinkled and he sat back in his chair with a thud. "But you hated one another."

Darcy closed his eyes briefly and took a deep breath. "I never hated her."

"But she must have hated you." Hurst pointed one finger at Darcy and shook it as he addressed the rest of the party. "Argued all the time, they did. Could not even make sense of it half the time."

"Then your money is on my brother?" Saye asked.

"This is not a matter to wager upon like some boxing match or a horse race," Darcy protested.

"Love is absolutely a horse race, and if you think it is

not, then you have been doing it wrong all along," Saye informed him loftily. "Shall I start a book on this, men?"

"What if," Fitzwilliam asked, "neither of us gets her?"

"Three outcomes, then. Even better."

"She did not suit *my* fancy," said Hurst, "but I say she was a fine filly. Good hair—and you know, the hair is the first sign of a woman who can birth easily."

"Old wives' tales," Saye said dismissively. "You in or what, Hurst?"

"Aye, and I shall put in a share for Bingley, too."

"Excellent!"

"You cannot do this," Darcy said. "I absolutely insist that you cease this nonsense at once. It is disrespectful to Miss Elizabeth and to her family. She should not have her future haggled over in this undignified manner."

"No one even knows who she is," Saye protested.

"But they will, will they not? If she comes to town as either my wife or his"—Darcy glared at Fitzwilliam—"they will understand it was she who was the object of all these wagers."

"And by that time, she will be either the daughter of an earl or Mrs Darcy, and no one will give a tinker's curse about some bets laid over her engagement," Fitzwilliam said.

"Come, Darcy. You know full well that the betting books are filled with things of this sort," Hurst added.

"This one is just more interesting because of the parties involved," Saye explained. "Cousin against cousin! A battle to the death!"

"Hardly a battle to the death," Darcy muttered,

though in truth the idea of Elizabeth married to Fitzwilliam did feel, at times, like it might kill him.

"When do we go, then?" Saye asked. "I should prefer to wait until after Lady Bainwright's ball."

Darcy and Fitzwilliam exchanged a look. It was dashed awkward—Bingley had been all but forced to offer Fitzwilliam an invitation to the wedding festivities, but Saye? Saye had no right cause to be there.

Happily, Fitzwilliam claimed a brother's privilege and spoke plainly. "You are not acquainted with the bride or her family, and have no reasonable expectation of an invitation."

Saye pressed a hand against his chest, feigning shock and outrage. "I know Bingley, do I not?"

"Bingley will not mind," Hurst offered. "You could bring twelve friends and he would be delighted."

"You dislike him," Darcy reminded Saye.

"I have no idea why you say that. Bingley can be a charming lad."

"I say it because you do not recognise him. You delight in very nearly cutting him every time you see him."

That made Hurst laugh.

"I should not say I *delight* in it," Saye replied. "I undertake it as my duty such that the distinction of rank may be preserved."

"And thus—why would he invite you to attend his wedding? A wedding in a place of no consequence where you would mix with people of little distinction."

"Because," Saye replied, drawing the word out, "I want to. Not only that, I am needed. Who else can oversee this contest? Someone must be there to ensure that fairness and honour are upheld."

Darcy rubbed a hand across his forehead. The headache which had been plaguing him since that night in the parsonage, when Elizabeth rejected him so scathingly, was making itself known with greater insistence. "It is neither my place, nor Fitzwilliam's or Hurst's, to issue an invitation to you."

"I do not need your invitation." On their looks, he insisted, "I do not! As the old proverb goes—everyone loves a viscount."

"What proverb is that, exactly?" Fitzwilliam asked with a laugh.

"None that I have ever heard of," Darcy grumbled. He wished he was as easy as Fitzwilliam, and could sit and listen to Saye's rattles and nonsense with a chuckle. Alas, he could not—not with the prospect of losing Elizabeth hanging over his head.

"Nothing is better than a viscount at the party. All the enjoyment of rank and wealth with few of the responsibilities of an earldom. A merry lot are we, and always welcome wherever we go," Saye informed them all with a royal flourish of his hand. "And that is just what Bingley wrote in reply to my note where I informed him that he would honour me greatly by inviting me to attend. It is all settled already, so your views on the matter are quite unnecessary."

It seemed there was nothing Darcy could do to stop this—not the contest, not the wagers, not even Saye inviting himself to a place he had no right to be, and would likely despise once he got there.

What a hypocrite I am, he mused, watching as Saye waved over the servant to bring fresh drinks. *Taking Elizabeth to task for the misbehaviour of her family when I am attached to people equally indecorous and, like her, can do nothing for it.*

Darcy stood up so abruptly it nearly sent his chair tumbling, causing his cousins and Hurst to stop talking and stare at him. "Monday, first light," he said tersely before taking his leave of them.

CHAPTER FOUR

Once Darcy had gone, a short silence fell before Hurst looked at Saye and said, "Must have been you, I suppose, who sent Bingley that fine Cognac he showed me last night?"

"I may know someone who gets it for me."

"Very handsome." Hurst made vague excuses about meeting people, clapped Saye on the back, nodded to Fitzwilliam, then left, likely going to the card room. Fitzwilliam knew no one who liked to gamble so much as Hurst and his elder brother did.

Once Hurst was safely out of earshot, Saye gave him an appraising look. "I cannot account for the fact that this hare-brained scheme of yours seems to be working."

"I am a strategist, big brother, through and through."

Saye scoffed. "Pray do not think that tottering about on a few battlefields makes you some expert tactician."

"One thing I can assure you of is that this play-acting business is far more difficult than ever I had supposed,"

Fitzwilliam confessed. "I cannot like how cruel I had to be to Darcy to properly goad him into action."

"Eh." Saye shrugged. "The two of you have always had the ability to fight viciously one minute and shake hands the next. I am sure he thought it no different."

"For the woman he loves? That *is* different."

"But he is not thinking of that. His only thought *now* is for winning her. It will not be until later that he might consider the cruelty of your actions, perhaps even doubt them. We can only hope that by then, he will be happily married and no longer care how it came about."

"And what if everyone learns that I never had any intention of marrying the lady?"

"What's that?" Saye asked. "I could not hear you."

"I said that… Oh. I understand."

"I am tasked with making the book, and I shall do so on my understanding that you do intend to woo the lady as mistress of Sapskull Hill, and when Darcy gets her—well, so it goes."

Fitzwilliam grinned. "I am surprised you wish to go to Bingley's wedding. You do realise Bingley's sister will be there?"

"Miss Bingley is not so bad on the eyes," Saye said after some thought.

"No, it is only when she speaks that she grows intolerable. Never mind that though, it will be Darcy who endures the first part of her attentions. Even with this mythological Snow Hill—"

"Salt Hill. Pray do remember the name of your own estate."

"Salt Hill, yes. Alas, even with Salt Hill, I am not nearly wealthy enough for Miss Bingley."

"But you are the son of an earl," Saye reminded him. "There is position to be had. Another reason I must be there—Miss Bingley and her like will be too much enchanted by me and the earldom to look your way."

"I am still surprised you mean to go."

"I did a bit of asking around, and what do you suppose I discovered?" Saye leant forwards. "Miss Lillian Goddard's family has a place not ten miles from these Bennet people."

"How does that signify?"

"I have decided I want her."

Fitzwilliam barked out a surprised laugh. "I do not recall any mention of her by Miss Elizabeth, so they might not be acquainted."

"That is nothing to me. They will all know one another well enough by the time we arrive at the breakfast."

"Impossible."

"Think so?"

"I do."

"Want to put some money on it?"

Fitzwilliam sighed heavily. "Twenty pounds says we shall not see hide nor hair of Miss Goddard in Hertfordshire."

Saye extended his hand, and the brothers shook. While they did so, another man arrived at the table. Sir Frederick Moore was Saye's particular friend and generally close by wherever the viscount happened to be. He stood with a tankard of ale in hand. "What is this I hear about a wager concerning Darcy?"

"Nothing to worry yourself—" Fitzwilliam began but was interrupted by his brother.

"You will love this, Fred. Both my brother and Darcy are chasing after a famed country beauty. You want in? I have a book going on it."

Sir Frederick was not invited to sit but sat regardless, sloshing drink over his hand as he did. "I shall throw in, but who is she?"

"You do not know her and probably will not until she is either Mrs Darcy or Mrs Fitzwilliam," Saye replied.

For some reason, Sir Frederick found this hilarious—evidently, he was more in his cups than Fitzwilliam had realised when he approached them—and laughed a loud, donkey's bray of a laugh that made several other men glance towards them. "Now *that* is a bet I am happy to lay," he bellowed.

He was so loud that several other men came over, wishing to know what scheme was ongoing. By the time an hour had elapsed, the bets were numerous. Saye gave Fitzwilliam a gleeful punch on the arm as he stood to leave. "We are going to make so much money on this," he hissed gleefully.

~

"Hurst! Is it true?"

Having been poised to enter his carriage, Hurst stopped and nearly groaned at the figure he observed trot-

46

ting to meet him. "What do you want? Where is my money?"

George Wickham approached, a little breathless. "I shall pay, you need not worry for that."

"I have been hearing that since last November."

"But is this thing with Darcy true? He and the colonel are vying for Miss Elizabeth Bennet?"

Hurst shrugged.

Wickham shook his head. "To imagine Darcy, of all people, falling in love!"

"Love? I said nothing of that."

"You do not have to say it. Nothing less than love could induce him to be so undignified. I want in."

"In?" Hurst quirked a brow. "It is a private little wager between friends. It is not open to just anyone."

"Come, Hurst!" Wickham took another step closer, and Hurst's nose wrinkled. Wickham smelt of cheap ale and desperation, two things Hurst hated. "Surely *you* have some money on this?"

"What if I do? Saye started a book, obviously I threw in," Hurst replied impatiently while looking at his horses. They were ready to move, and he did not like to leave them standing in the warm spring sunshine overlong. "If you have something in your pocket, you would do best to pay the people you owe, including me. More wagers can only sink you."

"Had I more of it, I would, but a fellow does need something to live on."

"Thought you were getting married?"

Wickham gave a little huff and flicked one hand. "It went off."

"She came to her senses, you mean. Or did her family put a stop to it? Ah, I understand now. They paid you to disappear. Hence the fullness of your pockets."

"The point being that sure wagers will do better for us all. If I can increase the sum—"

"That is the dream of every gambler, is it not?" Hurst enquired.

"This contest is one that will be easy to predict."

"You think so?"

"I *know* so." With a significant look, Wickham said, "Have I not known the gentleman in question my entire life long? And I am scarcely less friendly with the lady."

With an inelegant snort, Hurst said, "Any man who thinks he can accurately know a woman's mind is a fool. Besides, I do not think she likes Darcy. All they ever did was argue with one another."

"Mark my words, he will have her."

Hurst shook his head. "The colonel has a military man's mind for strategy, and he is tenacious. He will not lose."

"We must agree to disagree then—but pray do put something behind it, will you? You have my word, when I win, yours will be the first debt paid."

Wickham's voice had taken on a wheedling accent, another thing Hurst despised. He had enough of that from his wife and her sister. How he disliked consorting with these low types! It was always this arrangement and that, always granting a favour, always hearing this promise to pay and then another plea for more time. Excessively tedious. At once he was willing to do anything just to get away.

That said…he was clearly not going to get anything from the man otherwise. Might as well take what he offered, place the bet, and see what happened. "I want ten percent up front," he demanded. "Not towards the wager itself—pay to play."

Wickham frowned, so Hurst put a foot on the step that would get him into his carriage and said, "A good day to you, then."

"Wait!" Wickham heaved an enormous sigh. "Five percent?"

Hurst turned back, hand on hip. "Has your time in the militia damaged your hearing? Ten. Not a farthing less."

Another deep sigh ensued, but it was followed by the reluctant withdrawing of a purse from Wickham's jacket.

Hurst received the purse, opened it, and counted. A nice sum, but nothing to be overly thrilled about, not for a man like himself. He removed his due, returned the rest to the purse. "And you are *certain* you want to put the money on Darcy? I am telling you that I have been in company with the pair of them. They are barely civil to one another."

"Darcy will get what he wants—he always does," Wickham insisted.

I should have insisted on twenty percent up front. Hurst extended a hand and the two men shook. "A good day to you, then. May the best man win."

Wickham smirked. "Depend upon it, Hurst. As with everything, it will be the wealthy man who wins."

CHAPTER FIVE

Back in March, while she was yet at Hunsford Parsonage, Elizabeth Bennet had been delighted to receive a letter from Jane explaining that Mr Bingley—having learnt of Jane's presence in town by means that were unclear to anyone—had defied his family and friends and called on her at the Gardiners' home

Pray forgive me, dear sister, for keeping it from you, but I could not easily understand what he meant by calling on me in Gracechurch Street. His own sister had been so very definite on the point of his disinterest, and I was very afraid to allow myself to hope.

The letter went on to say that Mr Bingley had proposed. Several paragraphs of Jane's rapturous exclamations were included and made Elizabeth smile no matter how many times she read them. Given the timing of things, she wondered whether he had proposed on the very night of his friend's ill-fated addresses to her. *So, Mr Darcy did not, after all, ruin the happiness of a most beloved sister*, she mused. *But it was not for lack of trying.* Mr Bingley's will had prevailed.

> *Charles has gone to Hertfordshire to seek my father's permission and has said that—if she would like it—he will bring my mother to London when he returns. Dear Lizzy, pray tell me you will return to London too? You know I am always in need of your help to stand up to her when we shop.*

Elizabeth had found the notion of leaving Kent early a very agreeable one. Everywhere she turned was some recollection of Mr Darcy, and each recollection made her feel more and more ashamed of herself. She had been blind, partial, prejudiced, and absurd, happily surrendering to the lies of a man who flattered her and ignoring the goodness of the man who did not. *Who would have imagined me so vain?* She had hoped that the remembrances would not travel with her to London or, if they did, that the busyness of preparing for Jane's wedding would make it impossible to ruminate over them.

Once ensconced at Gracechurch Street, Elizabeth did her best to put aside condemnation of herself and plunge into the arrangements for dear Jane. She was a carefully careless chaperon when Mr Bingley came to call, and listened with endless patience to her sister's musings on love and her beloved when he was absent. Jane's happiness was the finest antidote to the misery within her own heart.

She lived in fear of meeting Mr Darcy in London; her only consolation was that he would avoid her as assiduously as she must avoid him henceforth. Jane's wedding did present some danger, for surely Mr Bingley would invite his friend to attend. She could only hope that Mr Darcy's dislike of the neighbourhood would keep him away.

"Now Lizzy." Mrs Bennet leant towards her second daughter in the carriage as they travelled back to Hertfordshire. "None of this running off into the fields when we get back. There is scarcely a fortnight! We must plan the breakfast, and arrange for…"

Elizabeth exchanged a small smile with Jane as her mother rattled away. More letters had gone between Gracechurch Street and Longbourn than either of them could have ever imagined, and she did not doubt that Hill had everything well in hand. Nevertheless, Mrs Bennet would go in and upend all the plans, insisting on the impossible and disregarding the probable. And Hill would be as wonderful as ever she was, simultaneously taking care of them all and soothing her mistress's nerves.

"Mama!" Elizabeth cried with a little laugh some minutes later. "I do not intend to run off. I am well pleased to be by Jane's side. Nothing less than perfection will do."

"I should think not." Mrs Bennet thudded back into the squabs with a sniff. "She is marrying a great man, you know."

"I do know." Elizabeth grasped her sister's hand. "And he is marrying a perfect lady. Jane, have I told you how happy I am for you?"

Jane turned pink with pleasure and lowered her eyes. "Only ten times a day, Lizzy."

Elizabeth squeezed her hand and let go. "Then make today's count eleven. I am so very happy for you, dear sister."

Even Mrs Bennet could think of no criticism in the face of such sisterly affection and only smiled. The congeniality among them lasted until the very moment they entered Longbourn's door. Hill came to greet them and received an immediate flurry of instructions, through which she calmly removed pelisses and bonnets and sent their maid, Sarah, off to gather refreshments for them all.

"Yes, yes, ma'am," Hill repeated over and over. "All will be well. 'Tis all in hand."

Mr Bennet removed himself from his book-room and came to kiss his wife's cheek and nod approvingly at his eldest daughters. "Well, Jane, Lizzy. Good to have you home again, even if Jane's tenure is to be short."

"Let us all sit," Mrs Bennet announced, "and then we may acquaint you with all of our plans."

"I daresay I am acquainted with them well enough," said Mr Bennet with a twinkle in his eye. "The bills have preceded you, my dear, although I should imagine a painful lot remain to come."

"Well," said Mrs Bennet as she breezed through the

vestibule on her way to the breakfast parlour, "Lizzy is intent on refusing offers of marriage, and Mary can scarcely be prevailed upon to dance with a fellow, much less marry one. We might as well extend ourselves for Jane!"

Elizabeth followed her sister and mother down the hall, thinking of what her mother would do if she had any idea of her refusing Mr Darcy.

It was not too much longer before they were enjoying an afternoon repast of cold meats and cheeses with bread and tea. Elizabeth longed to escape to the sanctuary of her bedchamber; alas, the rumbling of her stomach would not permit it.

Lydia entered the breakfast parlour in her customary high-spirited way, tossing herself into a chair and serving herself a generous slice of cake. "Such news, Mama! I could scarcely wait until you were home to tell you!"

Kitty entered behind her sister, subdued; her eyes were red-rimmed and her colour was high. She settled into the chair farthest from Lydia and said nothing, only looking sullen and put upon. Elizabeth groaned silently, wondering what argument had arisen between them now.

Mrs Bennet, busy buttering a piece of bread, asked without much concern, "What is it?"

Lydia sat straight, visibly preening as she announced, "Mrs Forster has invited me to Brighton as her *particular* friend. There will be balls and assemblies every night, and sea-bathing and card parties—"

"She ought to have asked me!" Kitty interrupted indignantly.

"You are not her particular friend," Lydia shot back immediately.

"Particular friend or not, I am two years older!" Kitty's eyes had already begun to well up.

Elizabeth glanced at her father, expecting him to say that neither of them would go, no matter who was invited.

"You will let me go, will you not, Mama?" Lydia entreated. "Papa says I am too young, but Mrs Forster has promised to take good care of me."

"Your sister's wedding!" Mrs Bennet reminded her. "How would it look if you were to miss the breakfast? And only imagine what rich friends Bingley might have invited to attend. You would not wish to miss that!"

"But after the wedding, the regiment will be gone and we shall all be dull and miserable," Lydia protested.

"Would you not take us all, Papa?" Kitty begged. "I do not think it fair that only Lydia should go."

"With the money being spent on this wedding," Mr Bennet replied drily, "I do not think I shall have enough remaining to get us farther than Watford."

Elizabeth smiled at the joke, the only person at the table who did.

"It would hardly cost anything at all," Lydia cajoled. "Lizzy, you will want to go most of all, especially when I tell you what I know about a certain person we all like."

Elizabeth reached to help herself to more of the salad. "Who might that be?"

"There is no danger of Wickham's marrying Mary King," Lydia pronounced. "She is gone down to her uncle at Liverpool; gone to stay. Wickham is safe."

"Perhaps it is Mary King who is safe," Elizabeth

observed mildly. "Safe from a connexion so imprudent as to fortune."

"Who cares about that?" Lydia replied. "Why are you not happier? I know you liked him."

Elizabeth pressed her lips together. The story Mr Darcy had disclosed was not hers to share, much as she should like to warn her young sister away from such a scoundrel as Mr Wickham. Even Jane knew only that Mr Darcy had proposed and been refused; what came after was not relevant. Elizabeth had no wish to relate a tale that could only distress her. But Lydia—apparently anticipating that her sister would be delighted to find her old favourite free, and incredulous that she remained sedate —wanted some answers.

"I am far less inclined towards the gentleman than you might have imagined," Elizabeth said eventually. "And in any case, what can it signify? He is gone to Bright—"

"Not yet," Kitty inserted. "He is part of the group that yet remains to break down the encampment."

That was unlucky. Elizabeth had hoped he would not be a part of the neighbourhood activities, of which there were to be many. "Well, he will soon be gone, and that will be that."

"Oh, enough about Mr Wickham! If that dreadful Mr Darcy had not denied him what he was owed, I should be very glad to see him married to any of you," Mrs Bennet cried. "But so it is not. Now once Bingley is officially your brother…"

With that, she was set off on the well-worn subject of suitors for the rest of her daughters. Mrs Bennet was certain that Bingley would very obligingly settle them all with one or another of his friends, and perhaps he would —save for one.

Strange how that thought gave Elizabeth a tiny pang of something like regret.

CHAPTER SIX

An hour later, the five Bennet sisters had gathered in Lizzy and Jane's bedchamber. Lydia's two eldest sisters were always so good, attending immediately to unpacking and distributing the presents they dutifully brought from London each time they went. Lydia might have hoped for something more than the fan she got—some muslin for a new gown?—but she would bide her time, hoping for more when she went to Brighton.

"There must be some way to make enough money to go to Brighton," Kitty said. "All of us."

"If there were any means by which such a sum could be earned so quickly, I am sure it would not be legal," Lizzy replied.

"I have plenty of money to go," Lydia reminded them all with a smirk. "A place to stay and a carriage to take me there."

Kitty sent her a very mean look. "That is very well for you, but for the rest of us—"

"Do you think Mr Darcy will come to his friend's wedding?" Lydia interrupted.

Lizzy coloured upon hearing his name and dropped her gaze. "I feel very certain he will not."

Now that is a very strange reply, Lydia thought, peering curiously at her. But Lizzy gave nothing more up than that.

Jane, from her seat at the dressing table, informed them, "Charles has asked him to stand up with him." Her eyes on her reflection, she asked, "Do you think I am getting a spot here?"

Jane poked at her flawless chin, and Lizzy assured her she was not.

"Likely from Bingley's chin whiskers!" Lydia teased, only to earn a censuring look from Lizzy. Well, for heaven's sake, Lizzy had to realise Jane was not marrying a man she had never kissed!

"I have a special remedy I use for mine," Mary announced. "Willow bark powder mixed with a touch of Papa's whisky. They just disappear overnight."

Do they? Then why do yours seem to linger about? Lydia barely stopped herself from saying so aloud.

"I shall go and get some," Lizzy offered. "I do not see any spot, but better safe than sorry."

In a trice she was gone, and Lydia returned to the previous subject. "Has Mr Darcy accepted?"

"I hope he does not," Kitty said. "He frightens me."

"I am not frightened of him," Lydia said. "I shall tell him directly to his face what I think of him for what he has done to poor Mr Wickham! Just see if I do not!"

"He told Charles he will stand up with him. Lydia,

pray do not make the man uneasy at my wedding." Jane gave her chin another poke. "I have not as yet told my mother, but evidently Mr Darcy's cousins will also attend."

"Who are his cousins?" Mary enquired.

"Colonel Fitzwilliam, who Lizzy says is very amiable —he was also in Kent—and his elder brother, a viscount and heir to the Matlock earldom," Jane replied. "Mama is sure to have vapours when I tell her."

"Our mother is so very certain that Bingley has enough wealthy friends to make husbands for us all," Lydia said with a giggle. "Would it not be hilarious if the viscount liked me? I should make you all begin to call me Lady Lydia straightaway."

"You may consider the viscount taken," Jane informed her. "Evidently he is quite in love with Miss Lillian Goddard, and I have invited her to come to the wedding on his behalf."

"Miss Lillian Goddard?" Mary asked. "Are you acquainted with the lady?"

"I know her a little, hopefully enough. Her parents have Ashworth," Jane replied. "She might think the invitation unexpected, but how could I disoblige the viscount?"

"Well, fie on him, then! 'Tis likely the colonel will be more to my liking any way," Lydia announced. "I would still be the daughter of an earl if I managed to secure him."

"I fear that is even less likely than the viscount," Jane said. "For the colonel has nothing of his own and is determined to marry a lady who has at least forty or fifty thousand—according to Lizzy. He was sure to warn her off straightaway."

Kitty gasped, as did Mary, who then recited some scripture about a man laying up his treasures in Heaven, which Lydia decided to interrupt.

"Then I shall just have to make an attempt on Mr Darcy. Can you imagine? That severe, tedious man falling in love with me?"

"The only thing less likely," said Kitty, "would be him falling in love with Lizzy."

That made all four sisters laugh. "I would bet you anything that I could make him kiss me," Lydia said. "Who wants to bet with me?"

"You should not be kissing anyone," Jane said primly. "Do remember that Mr Darcy is a very guarded man. He would never kiss a lady for mere silliness. He would likely think he needed to marry her afterwards."

"Exactly!" Lydia cried. "Imagine me, a great lady! Ooh, I like this idea even better than the scheme for the colonel. I am going to make Mr Darcy kiss me! Just you see if I do not!"

"Me too," Kitty replied. On her younger sister's look, she retorted, "By rights, I ought to marry before you do, Lydia! If Mr Darcy kisses anyone, it should be me."

"By that rule," said Lydia, "it ought to be Lizzy next, but we all know how much Mr Darcy dislikes her."

"Lizzy could earn Mr Darcy's kiss just as easily as the two of you, and perhaps more," Jane interceded staunchly. "Lest you both forgot—it was only Lizzy who danced with him at the Netherfield ball last November."

"That is true," said Mary. "But prior to that, he had refused to stand up with her at the assembly."

"Lydia, you would not wish to marry a man like Mr Darcy," Jane continued. "Think of the responsibility it would be, helping with his estate, caring for him, having his children..."

"Ugh!" Lydia shuddered. "Too true. Well then! Who wishes to bet we can make him kiss Lizzy before he departs Hertfordshire again? I shall put my new bonnet on it."

"I shall put in my lace gloves," Kitty said.

"I do not wish to give away my possessions," said Mary primly, "but I shall put a groat on Lizzy *not* being kissed by Mr Darcy."

A groat? Lydia nearly groaned.

"A half crown that Lizzy will be able to get a kiss from Mr Darcy," Jane said.

Just then, light footsteps were heard returning up the stairs and down the hall. Jane shushed them all, needlessly, just as Lizzy entered the room.

"It was not easy to get Papa to give up a bit of his whisky, but I managed to persuade him," she said with a smile. "Now, let's rid Jane of her imaginary spot."

CHAPTER SEVEN

"**D**arcy and his cousins will be arriving in time to dine at the Robinsons'," Bingley announced.

Elizabeth wondered at the frisson of energy when he said so; her curiosity could only increase when she believed she heard Kitty murmur, "Let the game begin," to a beaming Lydia. She had no idea what that meant but forgot it immediately. Her greatest concern was whether Mr Darcy would speak to her. Would he burn with hatred for her or be coldly indifferent? She was not sure which would be worse.

When the night of the party arrived, she was the first dressed and used the advantage to speak to her father privately. Lydia had grown nearly insufferable, incessantly boasting about her plans for Brighton. Elizabeth was increasingly worried that her father meant to let her go.

"Come in, Lizzy," said Mr Bennet. "Eager to get to the party, are you?"

Elizabeth paused to take an account of him. Her father often had strange ideas for evening attire. He felt that being in fashion was tedious and that his own innovations set him apart—which they did, but not always for the good. Tonight, he had chosen to wear a puce-hued cravat that he likely had dyed specially and which in no way matched the rest of his garb. She forbore mentioning it, however, wishing to delve into a more important matter.

"Eager for the party, yes, but also wishing to speak to you in confidence."

"Oh?" He poured himself a drink but did not offer her anything.

"You cannot mean to allow this scheme of Lydia's?" Elizabeth took a seat closest to the chair her father favoured for reading. "I cannot think it sound for someone of Lydia's age and high spirits to be in such a place with no one but a seventeen-year-old girl to chaperon her."

"Mrs Forster is seventeen, is she?" Mr Bennet chuckled, settling comfortably back into his own chair. "Colonel Forster is an old devil, to be sure. He is forty if he is a day, I would wager anything on it."

"But Colonel Forster has his own duties and an entire regiment that will engage his time and his thoughts."

"And why should he have uninterrupted peace to do so?" Mr Bennet was clearly in a mood to be sportive. "I say if he was fool enough to extend the invitation, let us punish him for it by accepting!"

Elizabeth smiled wanly. "There is real danger in such a place, danger to which Lydia, with her careless assurance and disdain of all restraint, will be particularly susceptible."

Her father was unconcerned, still easy in his chair with his drink, smiling at her worries. "Pray do not distress yourself so. She is too poor to be of much interest to these fellows."

Elizabeth cast her eyes skyward. *Too poor for matrimonial schemes, to be sure, but there are other men with more nefarious intentions, for which a lady's fortune is immaterial.* "I do not fear that she will come home married as much as I fear she might return irrevocably... harmed," she said delicately.

"Perhaps. But only think of this," Mr Bennet opined, clearly not understanding her meaning. "Until she is granted her way, there will be no peace in this house."

He was not incorrect. Lydia had thrown tantrums from the very day she was upright enough to be able to hurl herself to the ground in a fit of rage. "But are not some fights worth the battle?"

That made him frown. "They are," he said carefully. "And as her *father,* I have decided that this one is not."

Elizabeth recognised with dismay that she could not have secured Lydia's permission to go more firmly had she tried. In pleading against the matter, she had set her father so determinedly in his position that he would never be moved. As she watched him finish his drink, the words of Mr Darcy's letter came to mind.

The situation of your mother's family, though objectionable, was nothing in comparison of that total want of propriety so frequently, so almost uniformly, betrayed by herself, by your three younger sisters, and occasionally even by your father.

Those words had, on first read, made her burn with anger. Now she could not be so outraged. Alas, they had too much justice in them for true indignation. She considered whether she ought to be more frank with her father, more forceful in her opinions.

"Papa," she began, but Mr Bennet stopped her immediately.

"Now Lizzy, I have heard your opinion and shall take it under advisement. For now, we have a party to get to."

❧

Elizabeth was glad to have had advance warning of seeing Mr Darcy. She could not imagine what discomfort might have attended the surprise of seeing him enter Mr and Mrs Robinson's home. As it was, there was discomfort enough.

He arrived with Colonel Fitzwilliam and another man, whom she supposed must be the viscount, on either side of him. Mr Darcy looked half-ill, she thought, almost greenish. He certainly did not have the haughty air with which he had entered the assembly at Meryton last autumn. She almost pitied him, wondering what made him look as he did. *Surely not me,* she thought. *If anything, just the pure misery of having to associate with those beneath him.*

From the corner of her eye, she observed him. He went immediately to Jane and Bingley, as they stood with Mr and Mrs Robinson. He bowed over the hands of the two ladies and said something that made Jane blush and smile. He then shook hands with Mr Robinson. Elizabeth wondered what they were all speaking of. Mr Darcy's pallor was abating, and he appeared increasingly at ease standing with the couple he had tried so hard to tear apart.

"The famed Miss Elizabeth Bennet." A gentleman's lazy drawl jerked her out of her observations. She blushed to be caught staring at Mr Darcy, and then blushed still further as she had no immediate reply to cover her confusion.

To her great relief, Colonel Fitzwilliam arrived next to the gentleman only moments later. "A pleasure to see you again, Miss Bennet. When we left each other in Kent, I had not imagined I should have such an opportunity so soon."

"It is my pleasure as well," Elizabeth replied. "I am sure I had no idea of seeing you at my sister's nuptials, but we are delighted you are here."

"My brother here wishes to be introduced to you, if you would permit it?"

So this was—as she had expected upon first seeing him enter—the viscount who had sent her mother into raptures. Mrs Bennet had expressed boundless delight upon receiving the request to invite the sons of the Earl of Matlock to Jane's wedding. What followed was a flurry of additions to menus and arrangements that Mrs Bennet thought would make her parties the rival of anything the viscount had seen in London.

To add to such flutterings, Mr Darcy had reportedly, on his arrival, gone round to all those in the neighbour-hood. The explanation that he proffered for his largesse was to express his thanks for their generous hospitality last autumn and for seeing his friend so welcomed on his return. Mrs Bennet had, herself, been the delighted recipient of an Alençon lace shawl and fine-milled rose-scented soaps. Mr Bennet had been given some tobacco that he regarded satirically but enjoyed unreservedly. Mr Darcy's popularity within the region had thus soared, and scarcely could a conversation be heard that did not include some matron or another preening about her soaps.

Elizabeth gave the viscount a respectful curtsey as the colonel performed the introductions.

"Lot of handsome ladies here," Lord Saye remarked. "Am I to understand they are all your sisters?"

"Not all of them, no," she said with a smile, then gestured towards those with whom she claimed a true attachment, telling him their names. She managed, barely, to repress a wince as Lydia appeared to tickle Mr Denny as they beheld her.

"I must have you introduce me to your mother," Lord Saye proclaimed. "I am Romeo to Darcy's Mercutio, and your dear neighbours are charming to permit it."

Remembering Mrs Bennet's raptures over Mr Darcy's soaps made Elizabeth shudder—the attentions of the viscount could only incite worse. Pushing that aside for now, she enquired, "But do you, sir, have dancing shoes with nimble soles?"

His lordship looked at her quizzically. "What's that now?"

Elizabeth glanced uncertainly at the colonel, who informed his brother, "You just referred to a scene wherein Romeo goes to the Capulets' party and tells

Mercutio, I believe, that he has dancing shoes with nimble soles while he himself has a soul of lead."

"Well, lord, I do not have it memorised," Lord Saye replied with a sniff. "But I assure you, I have never had any complaints about nimbleness."

Elizabeth laughed. "And we are not feuding houses."

Colonel Fitzwilliam gave her a little wink. "Not yet. The night is still young."

"If anyone here has a soul of lead," said Lord Saye with a conspiratorial look, "it must be our cousin Darcy. Tell me, Miss Bennet, have you ever known anyone so gloomy at such a happy occasion? Surely there must be some way we can enliven him?"

Elizabeth's eyes slid towards Mr Darcy again. The Robinsons, Jane, and Bingley had left him, and he stood alone. His discomfort seemed to have returned in full measure; he lingered by the mantel, his eyes fixed on nothing and a slight frown on his countenance. With all the perverseness of mischance, he looked over at her just then. She quickly turned her attention back to the present conversation.

"Um," she said, reaching for her hair and twisting a curl by her neck around her finger. "Perhaps he is... um...hungry?"

It was a ridiculous comment, and she was immediately mortified for saying so. What *was* the source of Mr Darcy's misery? She did not imagine it truly was hunger. Was he so very unhappy to be present? If so, the cause was likely *her*.

"I understand he did not much make himself agreeable in his first visit to Hertfordshire," said Lord Saye.

"He may be feeling all the discomfort of prior associations."

The colonel gave his brother what he no doubt believed was a discreet elbow to the ribs; Elizabeth saw it clearly but was uncertain as to the meaning of it.

"I am sure Mr Darcy need not feel any discomfort," she said. "All of Mr Bingley's guests are very welcome."

"Some more than others, perhaps?" the colonel said. He had a knowing twinkle in his eye, though what it was he believed he knew was a mystery to Elizabeth. Were the Fitzwilliam brothers in their cousin's confidence? Elizabeth glanced between them, seeing nothing that gave her any indication.

Thankfully, dinner was called just then, and people sought their various partners to escort into the dining room. She observed Lord Saye being paired with her mother, which was polite but nevertheless concerning. Fortunately, it seemed her mother was too much in awe of his lordship to make much fuss. She had high colour but did not appear to say a word as Lord Saye rattled away beside her.

The dining table had been adorned with large arrangements of flowers, greenery, and candles. Mrs Robinson sat Elizabeth between her cousin Philips, lately down from university, and Mr William Goulding. Having known both all her life, the dinner passed quickly and with much laughter—even if she felt uncomfortably aware of Mr Darcy some places down between one of the Miss Longs and Miss Bingley. She chanced to glance at him now and again. Not once was his dark gaze upon hers, nor did their eyes meet. He was, it seemed, content to be speaking with his own two dinner partners.

I suppose he never did look at me to find fault, else he would still be staring, she mused. *Perhaps he looked at me because...* She did not complete that thought. It did not signify. Not now.

CHAPTER EIGHT

Following the dinner, the party repaired to the drawing room; the ladies first, of course, with the men about half an hour later. Elizabeth had spent the intervening time in a conversation with her mother and Mrs Robinson; both ladies had been impressed by the amiability and condescension of Lord Saye and wished to discuss it at length. Elizabeth only half-attended, her mind full of Mr Darcy and wondering whether he would speak to her when the gentlemen returned.

When the men began to enter in smaller groups, Elizabeth saw that Mr Darcy was not immediately among them. Colonel Fitzwilliam was, however, and she observed with pleasure that he was engaged in amiable conversation with Sir William and Mr Robert Lucas, though he left them almost immediately to come to her. She moved slightly to allow space for him on her settee.

"Sir William is a fine fellow," he said. "Indeed, I find all of your neighbours exceedingly agreeable."

"You are kind to say so," Elizabeth replied.

Cautiously, she added, "Sir William can be rather talk-ative on the subject of his knighthood."

"And why should he not be? An honour worthily bestowed. I am the furthest person from one who thinks an accident of birth is greater than a man who has earned his stripes."

"A generous view."

The colonel grinned. "Dare I hope you might reward my generosity with a song? Do say you mean to play for us all."

"Me?" Elizabeth exclaimed. "I-I had not—"

"I surely have not come all this way to be denied the pleasure of your singing."

"I do hope you did not come all this way on *account* of my playing and singing, sir," she replied with a laugh. "For you have already heard the fullest extent of my talent in Kent and cannot disagree that it was mediocre in the kindliest of terms."

"Nonsense!" he cried. "I thought it all a capital performance."

Over the colonel's shoulder, Elizabeth observed Mr Darcy entering the room. With great effort, she forced herself to meet the colonel's gaze. "My sister Mary is the musician in our family," she said with a little gesture towards her sister. "I do not doubt she will be soon at the instrument and reluctant to give way to anyone."

Leaning closer to her, the colonel said, "Darcy mentioned a particular song he heard you exhibit at…was it Lucas House? He was quite enchanted by it."

"Lucas Lodge," Elizabeth murmured, retreating just slightly.

He closed the slight gap she had created between them, saying, "Darcy is rarely awed by a lady's talents as he was by yours that evening. Perhaps you might play it now?"

Elizabeth wondered at the colonel's object. In some ways he seemed to flirt with her—he stood too close, and he flattered too much—but then again, he seemed to wish to forward his cousin. It was baffling.

"Oh, go on and play something, Lizzy," Mrs Bennet interjected from her chair on Elizabeth's other side. "Your voice sounds well enough—if you do sing loudly, no doubt they will not notice the mistakes in your playing!"

Mrs Robinson peered around her mama and said, "Do oblige us, Miss Elizabeth." Then, in a loud whisper, added, "We do not wish to disappoint our honoured guests! Miss Mary can play when you are finished."

"Precisely my thought, madam." Colonel Fitzwilliam leant forwards to bestow a charming grin upon the older ladies. "Being disappointed is the thing I like least in the world." He said so lightly enough that the two ladies laughed; while they did, he rose, offering Elizabeth his hand. "Come, I shall turn the pages for you, or fan you, or simply gaze admiringly upon your countenance—whichever you prefer."

Whether he meant to flirt or not, his bold behaviour continued as Elizabeth went to the instrument. She selected a song from the music laid there, explaining that, as it was nearly eight months since the party at Lucas Lodge, she really could not recall what she sang on that occasion. What she chose was a happy tune, not especially romantic, and easily sung and played—necessary, for her mind was on Mr Darcy, not the music. *Could he have, even then, been looking upon me favourably?* It cast many things in a far different light to imagine it so.

The colonel remained tightly attached to her, turning pages and murmuring occasional asides to her as she played. He seemed—rather strangely, she thought—to look over at Mr Darcy occasionally, almost as if he wished for his cousin to see him flirting with her. *He cannot know what happened at Hunsford*, she concluded, *for I cannot believe he would be so unfeeling.* Mr Darcy did not seem to notice his cousin's efforts. He had joined Jane and Bingley where they sat with Lord Saye, a silent presence among what seemed a lively discourse.

When Elizabeth had finished singing, Colonel Fitzwilliam pronounced her performance, "A delight in every way. Well worth the travel, I assure you."

"Thank you." She appreciated his good humour, but it was no balm for the odd pang of disappointment she felt that Mr Darcy would insist on ignoring her. *You once said you loved me*, she told him silently from across the room. *Is this how it is, then?*

You gave him every reason not to love you, she reminded herself. Such reflections, though apt, did nothing to dispel her ache.

"Shall I escort you over to your sister?" the colonel asked. "She seems to have been trapped by my brother."

Elizabeth smiled, although her heart was not in it. That tall, upright form prohibited her from going towards Jane. If Mr Darcy preferred to pretend there was no connexion between them, she would do likewise.

"I shall go back to my mother," she said.

As they strolled towards the other side of the room, Elizabeth recollected that she had heard something of the colonel inheriting an estate. "Tell me of your new home," she said with renewed energies towards him.

"Hmm?"

"I understand you have recently inherited an estate from an aunt. That is thrilling news."

"Oh, yes. Saint's Hill. Well, it's nothing to Pemberley, I can tell you that much."

"I am sure it is lovely."

"It is well enough," he said dismissively. "But Pemberley! Now that is something you should see! One of England's great houses, to be sure."

Elizabeth had to wonder at the oddness of him, being so disinclined to speak of his own estate in favour of Mr Darcy's. It occurred to her that perhaps he had not yet had occasion to visit his future home. She asked him a question to that effect, and he seemed relieved to confirm the truth.

"Never so much as laid eyes on it," he said cheerily.

"I do not think you told me what county it is in."

"Hertfordshire," he replied immediately.

"Hertfordshire!" She looked at him in amazement. "Is it nearby?"

"Oh! Did I say Hertfordshire?" He gave her a sheepish grin. "I meant Derbyshire. Quite near to Matlock, actually."

"How nice," Elizabeth said. Something in the conversation was puzzling to her. He seemed almost uninterested in what she should have imagined would be thrilling to him. And if his estate was so very near

Matlock, and the seat of a childless aunt—had he truly never been there?

It was peculiar, but she did not think it her place to remark upon it. Instead, she asked, "Will you give up your commission?"

"Oh no," he replied. "I am determined to be a major-general one day, or perhaps higher."

It seemed an uncommon choice to her, but what did she truly know of these military men? She puzzled over it silently as he rattled on about his hopes and future, neglecting entirely any mention of Saint's Hill amid his thoughts.

CHAPTER NINE

"**I** had imagined that you might at least *speak* to the lady, Darcy," Fitzwilliam said to him. "Saye, should we lay a bet on how long it might take for our cousin to part his lips?"

"I might have spoken more, were you not insistent on occupying the space next to her at every turn," Darcy retorted.

"I would not have you make it so easy for me to win this thing," Fitzwilliam said. "Try to exert yourself just a little, hm?"

Darcy removed his pocket watch from his waistcoat and noted it was not yet noon. "How many more times might I expect to hear these taunts about my silence? This marks thrice in under twelve hours."

"Leave off, Richard," Saye spoke up from his position lolling on the chaise longue. "I am feeling vexed by you and can only imagine that Darcy finds you equally tiresome."

"Speaking of tiresome people, I have it on good

authority that all of the regiment will soon be removing to Brighton, but as of now, some men remain...including our friend." Fitzwilliam gave Darcy a significant look.

"I heard some of the young ladies speaking of him at the party," Darcy replied grimly. "Still just as popular as ever."

"I do not doubt it. Nor do I doubt that he will be in attendance at the assembly tonight, giving the ladies one last time to admire him in his regimentals." Fitzwilliam took a drink of coffee. "I do not intend to let it dissuade me, but I should understand—as would Miss Elizabeth Bennet—why you perhaps might not wish to be in his company."

"Not on your life." Darcy scowled at Fitzwilliam. "I shall be there, depend upon it."

"No need to skewer me with your glare." Fitzwilliam held up a hand. "Only a kindly offer. I know how you loathe the man."

"And you do not?"

"'Course I do, but I tolerate him better."

"I can tolerate him well enough," Darcy replied shortly. "I should nearly guarantee that he will remove himself once he sees the pair of us enter."

It was to Darcy's good fortune that he laid no bet on that prediction. Evidently George Wickham considered the inducement of so many pretty young ladies—who fawned over him as if he were leaving for the continent, not the pleasures of training by the seaside—far more powerful than the appearance of two men who wished to flog him.

Wickham, naturally, would not dare approach either

Darcy or his cousin. Instead, he made a great show of being unperturbed by them. He was careful not to dance when the colonel did—that might have brought with it some unwelcome and unavoidable intercourse between them—but rather spent his time in a corner making love to whosoever found her way into his web.

Elizabeth, alas, did not appear to be immune to the blackguard's charms. She did not approach him but neither did she avoid him. She stood back, watching him as he talked and laughed on one edge of the ballroom.

Perhaps she is awaiting the moment that she might get him alone. No need to worry about Fitzwilliam, then, for it seems her mind is still on Wickham. Why does she persist in looking at him?

Darcy supposed she must not wish to compete with the other young simpletons who danced attendance upon George Wickham. A flush of disbelieving irritation heated his back and made his neck itch as he watched her surreptitiously watching Wickham.

She does *love him. Knowing the truth of his character has not dimmed her admiration.*

He had not truly believed it, not even when he wrote it in his letter, but if she could be thus entranced, despite all she now knew of the wretch, then it must be love. Nausea rose within his gut, and he had to look away.

When he returned his eyes to her, Elizabeth had moved position, slowly walking round a column. Darcy did likewise, keeping her within his sights. *Deuce!* She had moved to have an improved view of Wickham, and judging from the way she pressed her lips together and knitted her brow, she was not best pleased. Was she jealous?

At least it is not Fitzwilliam.

Darcy cast a look over towards where his cousin stood, also amid a gaggle of silly young things, enjoying himself immensely. At least if he lost Elizabeth to Fitzwilliam, he would know her life would be enjoyable. But no, she would surrender herself to the misery of marriage to a libertine. He shook his head, his vexation stoking itself into fury at her stupidity.

Wickham asked some young lady to dance and led her away; suddenly Elizabeth turned and was walking directly towards him. Before Darcy could stop himself, he stepped in front of her, arresting her progress.

"Mr Darcy!" She curtseyed but he, rudely, did not bow, choosing instead to loom over her.

"Did you even read my letter?"

"What?" She drew away from him, eyes wide. "R-read your letter?"

"The letter I gave you in the grove at Rosings." He stepped closer. "Wherein I laid everything out before you, everything about *him*."

She edged away from him, seeming alarmed. "Mr Wickham?"

"Yes, George Wickham!"

"Of course I read it," she said, sounding affronted.

"Then how is it that he still manages to capture your fascination? I thought you cleverer than to imagine a handsome face could prevail over ugliness of character. Did you think I was lying? My cousin is directly over there"—he stabbed his finger in Fitzwilliam's general direction—"should you want to consult him, as I said you could in my letter. He will confirm every particular."

Crossing her arms over her chest, Elizabeth took a deep breath. Her tone was even when she said, "I do not require verification, Mr Darcy. I believed every syllable of your letter from the first reading."

"Oh? You cannot deny your interest. You have scarcely been able to take your eyes from him."

He had angered her now; her eyes flashed when she looked up at him. "Yes, I am interested—interested in making sure my sister does not fall prey to him."

"Your sister?"

"Lydia." Elizabeth gestured towards one of Wickham's remaining coterie. "*She* takes an eager interest in him, and I am determined to keep her from harm. It was *her* I was watching. Not him." She flicked a cool glance towards Darcy.

Fury seeped away alarmingly quickly, to be replaced by abashed stupidity. "Oh."

They stood together in strained silence while the rest of the party laughed and cavorted about them. The musicians played some Scottish reel that had everyone else dancing about merrily. Darcy thought his spirits could not have been a greater contrast to it.

"I read your letter, sir," she said at length. "And certainly did not disbelieve you. I could not imagine you telling me such…about your own…in any case, I had no doubts as to the truth of it. Yet I did not think it my right to share it with any of my acquaintance, not even my own father, though I cannot help but think that if Mr Wickham's true character was known, he would not be received. But for now, he is, and I must resort to vigilance to keep my sisters from a dire fate, particularly as I fear my sister may be permitted to spend the summer in Brighton with the regiment."

Darcy nodded, numbly. "Forgive me for suggesting that you—"

"Were in love with that loathsome cur?" Another coolly resentful glance was directed his way. "Just so we are both in full understanding of the matter, I was not *ever* in love with Mr Wickham. Not before I knew his true character, and certainly not now. My education was disinterested, it is true, but I do still flatter myself that I am not an idiot. Excuse me, please."

She turned on her heel and very nearly collided with Fitzwilliam, who had approached them unnoticed. Needless to say, he was not backwards to any scene or situation that resulted in Elizabeth Bennet nearly landing in his embrace. "Ho, Miss Elizabeth! Steady on!"

"Forgive me, Colonel," she said, sounding subdued. Fitzwilliam glanced over her head at Darcy in query, but Darcy only looked away.

Recovering nicely into bonhomie and bluster, Fitzwilliam exclaimed, "I began to think you were hiding from me!"

"Hiding from you?" She tilted her head up at him. "I am in plain sight, sir, and standing next to your own relation. If my intention was to hide, I should have done a poor job of it."

"It must have been my eagerness for our dance that confused me," said Fitzwilliam with a chuckle. Then, to Darcy's dismay, he extended his arm to her. "Shall we?"

Darcy gave his cousin a tight, disappointed smile as Elizabeth took it. Then, with no more than a nod and another 'excuse me', they were gone to join the dancers.

Almost beyond his own volition, Darcy followed them at a distance, his jaw tight as he observed the easy conversation between them. He had not done well with his little fit of rage. Now here was Fitzwilliam, who had begun without disadvantage, plying her with every charm he had. The dance began and still they chatted amiably as they circled one another, laughing and talking as they went. His chest tightened. Was it all hopeless? It certainly felt that way.

CHAPTER TEN

"And how has your evening been so far? Enjoyable, I trust?"

The colonel smiled down at her as the first strains of the dance began. Elizabeth could have sworn he took extra care to make his eyes twinkle. He behaved so boldly, but she supposed it must be because she was the only person truly known to him, save for the Bingleys. She knew there was no real intent behind it but was excessively grateful that her mother, whose mind was almost frighteningly fixed on Jane's glory, had not seemed to notice the colonel's attentions.

"Very much so," she replied as she circled around him. "And you?"

"Oh, I am enjoying myself exceedingly. If I lived hereabouts, I daresay I should never go to town for all the diversion to be had right in my own neighbourhood!"

It was gratifying that he should think so. They separated for a short time as the pattern demanded. When they came together again, she said, "How charming it is that you and your brother, who are no doubt accustomed to the highest level of society, should be so easily entertained here in our humble town."

She found it amusing that the two Fitzwilliam brothers, sons of the Earl of Matlock, should be so kindly to those in Meryton while Miss Bingley acted as if she was stepping in manure every time she was forced to speak to anyone beyond her own circle.

"Where is my brother?" The colonel glanced about, his eyes resting on Lord Saye happily ensconced in a group that contained both Mrs Bennet and Lady Lucas. He chuckled softly.

"He has been so sociable to all of them," Elizabeth said. "They are much obliged."

"Do not think it is any great condescension on his part. He loves mothers."

They were again obliged to pause in conversation due to the demands of the dance. When they were again united, Elizabeth asked, "What is it about mothers that draws your brother so?"

"Saye always says that if you want the choicest cuts of meat, you ought to get friendly with the butcher."

"I am not sure I understand that," Elizabeth said with a little laugh. "Perhaps I would do best not to ask."

"Matrons can provide two things my brother loves—gossip and introductions to pretty young ladies. No doubt his pursuit of both is why he sits there."

"He will need to take care with my mother, then. I am surprised she has not yet put my youngest sister, Lydia, in front of him." Elizabeth sighed, glancing to where Lydia was teasing a group of young men, including some of the regiment. "Then again, he does not have a red coat, so she would likely not be interested. You, on the other hand..."

The colonel arranged his face into an almost comically suggestive countenance, his lips in a pouty smile and his eyes half-hooded. His voice was low and throaty as he said, "Your sister is a pretty girl, but my idea of beauty is a bit more womanly."

Elizabeth felt herself colour and willed it back, praying for herself to remain unaffected. Perversely, it had the opposite effect; rather than be subdued, her blush spread across her countenance like a roaring fire.

Her embarrassment was not lessened when he continued, "As is Darcy's. I once heard him say he could not comprehend these men who marry mere girls. No one ought to marry before the age of twenty, in my opinion. You are twenty, I believe?"

Elizabeth gave a discomfited nod, unsure as to the colonel's meaning. "I shall be one-and-twenty in a few weeks."

"An excellent age to marry," he said with a wink.

She gave him a thin smile in reply. "I have always believed marriage has more to do with finding the right partner than arriving at some particular age."

Thankfully, the dance moved them at that point, and the subject of marriage was left. When they came around again, Elizabeth very much wished to direct the conversation back to more neutral ground.

"Your observations on my sister's age are not amiss. My father thinks it sound to allow her to follow the regiment to Brighton, but I am not sure she ought to."

"Which of your sisters is she?" the colonel asked happily, recovering to his more genial aspect.

Elizabeth gestured clandestinely to where Lydia danced with Captain Carter. Unfortunately, just then her sister gave one of her open-mouthed, unrestrained laughs as she allowed him to pull her into his chest in a decidedly improper embrace. Elizabeth grimaced, wishing she had not directed the colonel's attention in that direction just then. "She is but fifteen."

"That is full young to be in such a place. No doubt your mother will go with her?"

"Lydia wants to go as the particular guest of Colonel Forster's wife." With a little frown, she added, "A lady who is only seventeen herself."

"Ah. Well, one can only hope for the best in such cases."

The colonel did not seem unduly concerned. Then again, why should he? Lydia was no one to him. Though, having had his own experience with a young lady of fifteen left unattended at the seaside, she would have thought he might have more to say about it.

"I believe I heard Lord Saye mention that you had a younger sister?"

The colonel nodded. "She is married now and has lately had a daughter. It does not seem so long ago that she was causing us all similar worries over where she went and whom she was with."

"Did she give you much cause for alarm?"

"No, not really. Aurelia is the spirited sort, it is true, but she is the daughter of an earl and the sister of a military man. Then there is Saye, who likes to boast that, by virtue of his less seemly connexions, he could send a note at breakfast and have anyone at all murdered before it was time to dress for dinner."

Elizabeth laughed with shock. "Surely he speaks in jest?"

"One never knows with Saye. But taken altogether, it was protection enough for Aurelia to be safely settled without incident."

Elizabeth smiled faintly, her mind busily contrasting that with her own situation. Lydia had no brother—one who could order a murder or otherwise—and her father was not only *not* an aristocrat, he could scarcely be prevailed upon to look up from his book.

"I think I should speak to my father again and urge him to—" she began but the colonel interrupted her.

"I wonder, Miss Elizabeth, if you have any favourite walks hereabouts?" He leant in, his eyes again seeming determinedly piercing and twinkly. "I have missed our conversations in Kent."

If you miss our conversation so much, why not allow me to finish my sentence? She could say no such thing, naturally.

"I have many favourite walks," she began but then stopped. Somehow the idea of the colonel and his discomfiting stares and comments intruding upon her time was not enticing. They had been good friends in Kent, but now, when any chance remark might be met by some advance, he was less agreeable to her. *Perhaps I am too peevish?* She decided she did not care if she was.

"Regrettably, my mother has forbidden me to walk these days." She gave him an apologetic smile. "She

93

thinks every waking moment ought to be dedicated to Jane's wedding."

His attention was partly elsewhere, she observed; turning, she saw that Mr Darcy had drawn near, perhaps even close enough to overhear their conversation, and something in the tilt of the colonel's head suggested he was aware of his cousin's movements.

He was ostensibly listening to her reply, but evidently he had not listened closely enough for, returning to her with one of his meaningful stares, he said, a trifle loudly, "Splendid! I always enjoy a morning walk myself, so perhaps I might meet you one day."

"I am doing as much as I can," Fitzwilliam told his brother a short time after his dance with Elizabeth. "You should have heard me—I was all but shouting at her about taking walks in the morning, trying to give him a hint."

"Did he hear? These blasted musicians are nearly making me deaf." Saye grimaced. "I am unaccustomed to small ballrooms."

"The music does seem louder, does it not?" Fitzwilliam thought about it. "I believe he heard me but I cannot be sure."

"I suppose we shall find out tomorrow morning, if he appears from an early morning ride or walk of his own. You will not find me traipsing about the countryside at dawn for a woman, I shall tell you that much."

"Not even if Miss Goddard were in the habit of a morning ramble?"

"I do not need to rely on chance in that quarter." He smiled smugly. "Bingley had not yet given her an invitation to his ball, so I told him I would very obligingly take it to the Goddards myself."

"How good of you," Fitzwilliam said with a laugh. "In the meantime, do you not think it would be a handsome gesture to dance with your hostess?"

Miss Bingley had followed Saye hopefully all night. She had looked meanly put upon when he danced with Miss Bennet and Miss Elizabeth, but had seemed on the brink of apoplexy when he surrounded himself with matrons for the remainder of the evening.

"To dance with Miss Bingley would give her expectations," Saye replied. "She is just that sort. I could not so cruelly disappoint her. You and Darcy both danced with her. I daresay that is enough."

From the window, they saw Saye's carriage being brought up. "Go and get Darcy, will you? I expect he will have had enough of this too."

Fitzwilliam glanced to where Darcy stood, eyes still fixed on Miss Elizabeth, who was, even then, dancing with one of her local friends. "Is he ready to depart, do you think?"

"If he has not gathered up bollocks enough to ask her yet, then I doubt it will happen in the last gasps of the evening," Saye replied. "Let us get him home to bed so he can be awake early for his walk."

∾

"She argued with him," Mary reported later that evening. As was her custom, she had not danced at the assembly. Her evening was spent in a chair at the edge of dance floor, quiet and overlooked and happily quite near to where Lizzy and Mr Darcy had feuded. "He thinks she's in love with Mr Wickham."

"See? I did too," Lydia crowed from where she lolled on her bed in her chemise.

"She is definitely *not* in love with Mr Wickham," Kitty asserted while handing her brush to Mary to attend to her. The three girls were busily helping one another undress as Sarah, their housemaid and sometimes lady's maid, was busy with Jane and Lizzy. "She refused to stand up with him."

"She did?" Lydia asked with surprise.

"Well, in fact what she did was stop him before he could ask her. Vastly clever of her! Because otherwise she would have had to sit out. So she held up one hand and said, 'Mr Wickham, I pray you would not importune me by asking me to dance,' and then he said something I could not hear and she said, 'if you do not want certain personal matters bandied about in this room, I beg you to leave me at once.' What personal matters do you think she meant?"

"Nothing, I am sure," Lydia replied dismissively. "What could she possibly have on Mr Wickham? Any way, it does not signify, for she did not dance with Mr Darcy either, and we shall need at least that much for them to kiss."

"They walked in Kent," Mary reported. "In the mornings sometimes. Lizzy thought it was all the perverseness of mischance, but I wonder?"

"You think he tried to meet her intentionally?" Kitty asked.

"I understand that Rosings Park is quite large—larger even than Netherfield. It seems a small chance they would continually encounter one another by accident."

"Then perhaps we ought to try and make them meet each other on walks," Lydia said slowly. "Mary, you should go to her now and see if you can persuade her to go on an early morning walk with you."

"Having me there defeats the object."

"Well, I know that, of course!" Lydia huffed loudly. Lord, but her sister needed *everything* explained to her. "When morning comes, make some excuse—too tired, could not sleep, throat hurts, anything! Then she is off alone and hopefully will meet Mr Darcy!"

"Of course." Mary nodded. "While I cannot like lying to her, sometimes it can be needful." She slid off the bed and went to the door. "I shall go and speak to her about it now."

CHAPTER ELEVEN

"I heard a report of a most alarming nature."

Charles's blue eyes were fairly sparking with rage. Louisa Hurst glanced uncertainly between him, her sister, and her husband, wondering whether Caroline had done something wrong at the assembly the evening prior. Probably not—Caroline seemed to have a pious air about her. Her husband was unperturbed.

"What is it?" Hurst asked.

"I have learnt that there are wagers all among the regiment about Darcy and the colonel chasing after Elizabeth Bennet. And that you, Hurst, are a party to them." Charles drew himself up, and Louisa was reminded of how he had been as a child—small, sweet, and undeniably adorable on the few occasions he was roused into indignation.

"I think it is disgusting," Caroline said primly. "I refuse to believe Mr Darcy would willingly involve himself in such a thing."

Louisa smothered a smile. If the wager had not

involved Mr Darcy, Caroline would have been right in the midst of it. The very gown she wore that morning was purchased with her winnings from gambling at Lady Farnworth's last card party.

Hurst shrugged. "You know how it is. Two men, one lady—everyone wants a hand in how it might turn out."

"But her reputation!" Charles said angrily. "What of—"

"What of it? Pursued by two men above her station?" Lord Saye had entered the breakfast room. "Forget reputation, she will have renown."

That made Charles appear unsure. His lordship sank into a chair and Caroline immediately rose to serve and dote upon him. *You do not stand a chance, Sister*, Louisa thought, *no matter how much coffee you pour him.*

"One of them is sure to propose, you know," Lord Saye added.

"Impossible," Caroline declared. "Perhaps the colonel? But no, surely not."

Charles scratched his head. "I must agree with Caroline. I did not think Darcy even much liked her."

"Then it is a good thing I put your money on the colonel." Hurst smiled genially and gave Louisa a little sidelong glance.

"You did?"

"He did not wish to leave you out," Lord Saye reported from his chair. "So your money is on my brother for now, though you might change it if you wish to."

"Do not change a thing, Charles," said Caroline. "I am quite sure that Mr Darcy—"

"Strange of Darcy to be mixed up in this sort of thing," Charles said thoughtfully.

"Darcy started the whole thing himself. Has a new carriage riding on the outcome." As Lord Saye spoke, he removed a small flask from his jacket and dosed his coffee with it.

Seeing Louisa observing him, he winked and said, "My personal physician has me on a very strict regimen. Purely medicinal."

"What ails you, sir?" Caroline asked, suddenly all concern.

"*Horribili sobrietate*," Lord Saye informed her, causing Hurst to bark out a laugh.

Unlike her sister, Caroline had never studied her Latin and thus had no idea that Lord Saye had just said he suffered from sobriety. She nodded, her face a picture of sympathy, and said what a brave man he was to be in such good humour despite his struggles.

On the other side of the table, Charles still seemed to be weighing the bets.

"My money is on Mr Darcy," Louisa told him helpfully. "But mostly because I think these Bennet girls are grasping."

He scowled at her, and Louisa belatedly remembered that the reason they were all here was because he was about to *marry* a Bennet sister. "Save for dear Jane, of course."

"The colonel does seem friendlier with Lizzy," Charles said slowly. "I do not think I have seen Darcy so much as speak to her."

"I have put my money on the colonel as well," Hurst

told him. "A safer choice, to be sure. Truth be told, there are only a handful who believe Darcy will get her."

"Not me," Caroline said hotly. "It is impossible in every way."

"Whom do the odds favour?" Charles asked.

"Colonel Fitzwilliam," Hurst replied.

"Lord Saye, you must have placed your money on your brother?" Charles asked.

They all looked at Lord Saye, who only winked and smiled. "I cannot disclose the nature of my wager."

"No? Your money is on your cousin then, is it?" Charles pressed him, but the viscount would neither confirm nor deny. It was telling enough that he would not disclose his leanings; Charles gave a little nod. "Change my wager, then. My money is on Darcy."

The door opened then, and the very gentleman they had been speaking of entered the breakfast room.

"There you are, Darcy," Lord Saye exclaimed, sitting up. "Been for a walk this morning, eh?"

"At this hour?" Mr Darcy asked. "I am afraid not. I have not slept well."

What Louisa could not account for was why the viscount seemed disappointed by that.

The tightness in Darcy's chest, first experienced while watching his cousin dance with and romance Elizabeth, remained the next evening when he found himself at a large dinner party at the home of Mrs Susan Simpson. Fate's only concession to him was that he escorted Elizabeth into dinner. Alas, she barely looked at him during the short walk, and murmured a near-inaudible thanks when he helped her sit. Darcy managed to restrain a groan at seeing Fitzwilliam, a cocksure grin on his lips, take the place on the other side of her.

"Miss Elizabeth," he said. "A pleasure! You know, I have been thinking about what you said about…" With that, his cousin was off and running.

It should have been Darcy's duty to help serve her, and yet his cousin encroached upon even that, talking and laughing with her all the while.

His cousin had a little trick he liked to use with the ladies. He lowered the volume of his voice such that whomever he spoke to was required to lean closer to hear him—preferably displaying the tops of her breasts as she did. Elizabeth had, unfortunately, fallen prey to this little ploy and was nearly in Fitzwilliam's chair. Darcy turned his gaze to an intent study of his plate to avoid having to watch his cousin's lovemaking.

The meal might have been delectable, or it might have been detestable; Darcy could scarcely taste it. In truth, he doubted he would be able to name one dish served once he left the table, for none of it made any impression upon him. The only thing that did was the sure knowledge, which grew ever more sure, that he was losing. Nay—that he had already lost.

"I begin to think you do not care for your food, sir." A voice—*her* voice—intruded into the fog of despair in which he had encased himself.

"I beg your pardon?" He raised his eyes and looked at her.

Elizabeth was lovely in a rose-coloured gown that set off her complexion beautifully and with a twinkle in her eye that was no doubt a remnant of whatever nonsense Fitzwilliam had spewed at her. Never mind that, he had her attention now and he would soak in it.

She gestured towards his plate, which contained a lemon cheesecake. "You have barely eaten a morsel, and your dessert is untouched."

"Yes, oh. I, um...I ate a lot earlier."

"Did you?"

Determined to do better, he added, "The meal is delicious in every respect. I have always been more fond of English cooking than French."

"Have you?" She took a small bite of her own cheesecake.

"Um." He reached for his wine and took a drink to stall for some time. In truth, he was a man who ate what was placed in front of him and rarely gave much thought to what style it was, or how it was seasoned, or sauced.

Elizabeth's eyes were unwavering upon him, which did nothing to ease his present anxiety. Thankfully, she rescued him from her query. "Not that I have much experience in the way of French chefs, but I, too, prefer simpler fare. It likely speaks to my country-town indifference or whatever it was Miss Bingley accused me of."

The last was said with good humour, but it gave him a jolt. Well did he recall that conversation at Netherfield last autumn. Miss Bingley had begun to abuse Elizabeth almost before the door closed behind her. He remembered admitting that he should not like his own sister to make any such exhibition, but he had not meant it as censure.

Elizabeth could not have known that, however. He wondered when it was that he would cease finding further examples of his dreadful behaviour.

"I must be guilty as charged as well," he said. "Some well-roasted venison or beef and a nice potato is truly all I need."

"Your cook must be very grateful to you for it."

"I think that must be in part the reason for my preferences. As a boy, I often would sneak down to the servants' hall while they had their meal. It was always so jolly down there, all of them talking and laughing."

She nodded. "I have always thought it diverting to be below stairs as well, though Hill rarely allowed us to linger about. One quiet boy is likely far less disruptive than five boisterous little ladies all bent on stealing biscuits."

"I cannot deny that, though for my part there were generally two of us, not only me."

She, caught mid-sip, gave him a quizzical look over her wine glass.

"George Wickham," he said ruefully. "We were thick as thieves in those days."

"Oh, of course." She set her glass down, then turned towards him a bit in her seat, her head bent. "I am glad you mentioned him. I have wished to tell you how embarrassed I am by how I defended him to you. I-it was idiotic of me to believe his lies, so wholly—"

"No, no," he said. "He has the gift of pleasing wherever he goes. I cannot censure you for being charmed by him in the same way countless others, including my own family, have."

"He appealed to my vanity." She gave him a sidelong glance. "I should not have imagined myself so cheaply enticed, but so it was. I know better now how one man might take on the appearance of goodness while another..."

"While another comports himself as the villain?" Darcy offered a tentative smile.

That made her smile, faintly. "I did not say you were a villain."

"Your friends and neighbours did not think well of me last autumn," he said lightly. "I cannot blame them. I did not give you, or them, any reason to think well of me."

"Any man who commits the unpardonable sin of leaving a lady to sit at a ball is rather doomed, is he not?" She grinned. "Of course, I do not expect more invitations to be forthcoming. I was hardly an agreeable partner at Bingley's ball last November."

"You were perfectly amiable," he protested.

"Oh no." She shook her head, ringlets bouncing. "No, I was determined to punish you for what I believed was your cruelty to Mr Wickham. I behaved abominably, I admit it. But it has left me to wonder..."

"What?"

"Is it dancing itself that you find disagreeable? Or is it partnering with me that you find distasteful?"

On the surface, her countenance appeared light-hearted. But in her eyes was something else—perhaps worry? He knew not if he dared believe it. To imagine she might think that their last dance together had soured him on dancing with her! He *longed* to dance with her; it was no more than his diffidence where she was concerned that inhibited him.

"I am not overly fond of dancing, in truth," he said cautiously. "But I enjoyed dancing with you before, and I anticipate that I shall enjoy it again at Bingley's next ball if you would so honour me."

"I would like that," she said softly with a small nod. Amid nodding, however, she grimaced. Reaching behind her, she tugged at one of her curls at her nape.

"Is something wrong?"

"This always happens," she explained with a little wincing smile. "My hair gets entwined with my button, and it feels like half my scalp is about to be torn off with it."

She had her hand behind her but did not seem to make progress in terms of solving her dilemma, not if the frowns and pulls she made were any indication.

"May I be of service?"

"Would you?" She looked relieved.

He laid down his fork quickly, then wiped his hands on his napkin. "Of course."

She turned so that her back was to him, then reached up, pulling as much of her hair away as she could and exposing the length of her pale neck. He closed his eyes against the rush of desire that engulfed him—he could too easily imagine himself unfastening these problematic buttons even as he ran his lips over her nape—but then opened them again and set to work. She smelt delightful, sweet and floral and decidedly feminine. *Good lord, stop before you embarrass yourself!*

"What is it that you find to dislike in dancing itself?"

Elizabeth asked him as he gently unwound the hair. "It can be undignified, and if your partner is the tedious sort, it is nothing short of agony."

"Nothing like that," he said, undoing a particularly tightly wound strand. "In fact, my feelings on dancing trace back to when I was only sixteen or seventeen years old."

"Oh?"

"I had grown quite a lot that year," he told her just as the last bit of hair came free. "Seemingly overnight, although I am sure it was not so. Suddenly it felt like I had a lot more elbows and knees to account for than previously. My father thought dance instruction would help me, but in the event, it did quite the opposite."

She turned back to face the table with a smile of thanks. "Did it?"

He smiled faintly, remembering his younger self's humiliation. "The dance master told me that he had never been so fortunate as to go to the African savannah but that I had given him as good a view of a giraffe cavorting about as he would likely ever see." He smiled at her to show her it was an old embarrassment, and she laughed accordingly.

"Those childhood hurts do leave a mark, do they not? I can still recall when my father told us of Mr Benjamin Franklin's kite experiment. He said that the hemp strands on the rope of his kite stood on end with the electric charge travelling through it and Jane exclaimed, 'it must have looked like Lizzy's hair!'"

Darcy gasped but managed to turn it into a chuckle,

unable to imagine the very sedate Jane Bennet ever exclaiming anything, much less such an unkindness.

Elizabeth seemed to have read his mind. "Sisters are always capable of injuring one another, but in this case, I laughed and Jane cried, dismayed by her own cruelty. But the fact is, she was not incorrect. If it is not dressed properly, my hair can be quite wild—as you have just learnt first-hand—and back in those days, I would not sit still long enough for more than a plait."

"I think you have the most beautiful hair I have ever seen." His compliment was blurted out in the most inelegant manner imaginable and he reddened slightly at his own stupidity. "Fitzwilliam once told me that his sword was less sharp than my nose."

"Your nose?" she cried out. "But it is a fine, noble sort of nose!"

"It was far less noble on the face of a twelve-year-old, I assure you."

That made her laugh heartily, and he thought how strange it was to be hurling insults at himself so willingly. *Anything to hear her laugh.*

"My sisters used to say that I had such a boyish figure, they ought to dress me in breeches and pretend I was my father's heir," she told him.

Happily he stopped himself before uttering some inappropriate, albeit truthful, remark admiring her figure. "Um…my cousins teased me for my thinness as well," he confessed. "Saye always wanted to see whether I could fit into things—cupboards and barrels, one leg of a pair of old breeches we found once. I once got stuck in a hollow log they made me climb into."

She shivered. "Dreadful! I cannot bear small, confined spaces."

"Then I shall not even dare to mention the spiders to you," he said gravely.

"I have always liked spiders. Is that terribly odd for a lady? I used to cry when Hill killed them, and made her carry them gently outdoors instead."

He laughed and admitted, "I shall not lie, Miss Elizabeth—that is peculiar."

"You begin to see why my mother has always despaired of me," she said with a cheerful sparkle in her eyes. "A frizzy-headed moppet with a fondness for spiders."

"I find it charming," he said quietly, but it might have been lost in the rustling about the table. Mrs Simpson had risen to withdraw with her lady guests. As was proper, the gentlemen, Darcy included, also rose and assisted the ladies in their leave-taking.

Elizabeth hurriedly dabbed her lips with her napkin then laid it on the table and stood, picking up her gloves as she did. "Until next time, sir."

"Next time what?" Fitzwilliam pressed himself into their tête-à-tête. "Miss Elizabeth, what nonsense is this rapscallion tasking you with?"

"Nothing at all, sir, only speaking of spiders and the African savannah." She gave Darcy a little private look that was thrilling, then left them.

CHAPTER TWELVE

"The African savannah?" Fitzwilliam asked, but Darcy would not gratify his curiosity. He only shrugged; he much preferred to lose himself in recollections of the scant time he had spent talking to Elizabeth and the brief but glorious moments spent touching her, helping her with her small problem.

Thinking of that reminded him of another problem that plagued her—her young sister being permitted to go to Brighton with the regiment. She had mentioned it to him, and he had overheard her speak of it to Fitzwilliam; he had also heard bits of it himself in various conversations.

Mr Bennet was the picture of a gentleman at ease at the end of the long table, a glass of port in front of him as he chatted with Mr Simpson and Sir William Lucas. Beholding them, Darcy felt a pang of guilt. Yes, he had saved the Darcy name, but what of these other men, with their daughters, who had no idea what George Wickham was? Everything they allowed for Wickham—to dine in their homes, to dance with their daughters, to be received by their wives—was because Darcy had kept the man's true nature hidden from them.

In the end, the confession was almost fated, such was the arrangement. Mr Bennet's companions left him while he remained seated, obviously not eager to return to the ladies.

Darcy rose with his cousin, then said, "I shall be a minute," and gestured to him to go on.

Elizabeth's father seemed surprised when Darcy asked whether he might join him, but he nodded and offered the port from the decanter that rested by him. "Nights at the Simpsons' run long. Best to keep your glass full." He poured them both a generous glass, then took a sip and regarded Darcy curiously, no doubt wondering at his sudden wish to speak to him.

"I understand," Darcy said, after a sip from his own glass, "that Miss Lydia will be off to Brighton after the wedding."

"She will," Mr Bennet agreed with a nod. "Jane will be at Netherfield, Elizabeth intends to travel with her aunt and uncle, and Lydia will go to Brighton. If I can think of any place to send the other two, I surely shall. A summer of peace sounds just the thing after all this wedding business!"

A laugh was expected and duly given. Darcy then cleared his throat and said, more seriously, "Loath as I am to disturb your plans, there is something I wish to acquaint you with before she goes," he began slowly. "As you know, I have a younger sister, and last year when she was fifteen, I was prevailed upon to allow her to go to the seaside with her friends and…and it had near-disastrous consequences that I have kept…quiet…for the sake of my name. Alas, I am just now recognising that silence and secrecy exposes other young girls to the same danger."

"What danger do you mean?" Mr Bennet asked.

Mr Bennet received the information about George Wickham as well as Darcy could have hoped. He could only pray the gentleman would act in the best interests of his daughter.

He could not be surprised to see that Fitzwilliam had attached himself to Elizabeth in his absence. Saye was also in the small knot of people with her, as was Miss Bingley, who was taking on a great deal of importance from having such intimacy with a viscount. Darcy considered pushing himself into the group, but it would not be easily done. He would need to drag a chair to where they all sat, and it would be awkward, to say the least.

You want to show her you attended to her reproofs, he reminded himself. *Start by being kind to her neighbours.* How well he recalled her words the night at Rosings when he had so foolishly imagined her to be flirting with him, refusing to hear the censure in her words!

"Shall we ask him why a man of sense and education, and who has lived in the world, is ill qualified to recommend himself to strangers?"

"I can answer your question," Fitzwilliam had said, *"without applying to him. It is because he will not give himself the trouble."*

Well, he would now. He would 'give himself the trouble' for her. Looking about the room he espied a young gentleman standing alone near the mantel. There was something familiar in his air, or perhaps it was his looks, that seemed genial and intelligent, so Darcy decided to go over and speak to him.

"How do you do?" Darcy said as he arrived next to him. He introduced himself, worrying briefly whether he presumed too much to imagine himself socially superior to the fellow. *Then again, were he a man of consequence, I would likely know him already.*

The young man informed him that he was Mr Philips, 'the cousin of the bride' and recently down from Oxford. Darcy extended his hand, and they shook. "Will you study the law? I believe your father is a solicitor?"

Philips grimaced. "That he is, and my grandfather before him. He and my mother would enjoy nothing more than if I did that, though Meryton and its businesses can scarce support one solicitor, much less two. In truth, I have not much affinity for the law."

"I have often envied those who have the liberty to consider their own preference in such things." The boy looked at him curiously, so Darcy continued, "As the heir to an estate—which is an honour and privilege, of course —my future has been pre-ordained. Do not think me ungrateful, I beg you, but I have before wondered how it might be to consult my own talents and preferences."

"My father has little for me to inherit, but his opinions are no less strong for it," Philips replied with an amiable grin.

"What would you do, were you left to your own wishes?"

"A few fellows and I at university set ourselves up with a small business of our own. It was slow going at first, particularly for those of us with little to our names, but we have built up enough interest now that we might make a go of it."

"A shop?"

Philips shook his head. "More of an investment... group. A partnership, so to speak, among many and varied partners."

"I am not sure I follow you."

"See, it works like this: many times one sees an investment that is perhaps less assured than another might be—but one which yields a higher possible return."

"Many a fortune has been lost on just such ventures," Darcy observed.

"Just so. What my friends and I began to do was put together groups of people, those who might be tempted into higher risk sorts of ventures. Then each of us put a smaller amount in. Then we split the profits—or losses, if it comes to that—between us all. So no one loses a great deal, no matter what happens."

"But no one gains as much either."

"Unless one measures the gains against another, less profitable, investment. If you were to invest fifty pounds in something secure, knowing you would earn sixty in return, that would be excellent. However, if you could enter one of these schemes with your same fifty pounds and return one hundred—even if it were only part of five hundred, for example—you would still have gained." Philips smiled. "But I do not explain it nearly as well as my partner Millard does. He's the one who goes about explaining the opportunity to people, gathers up investors."

A footman came by just then with some coffee. Darcy took one almost absently, his thoughts absorbed by the scheme Philips described. "Who else do you have in it?"

"There is Beaumont—he specialises in finding the investment opportunities. Has a good nose for them too. Langley is our accountant. Just loves to make sure all the farthings are accounted for."

"And what is your part in all this?"

"I help Beaumont seek out opportunities and I suppose you could say I weigh those opportunities," Philips told him. "We do not pursue just *anything*. Our specialty is finding opportunities that *appear* risky but are perhaps less so upon closer examination."

"How so?"

"There is risk, and then there is… I suppose you could say less risky risk." The younger man chuckled. "Pure luck is much less a factor than many people suppose it is. For most things, one can reasonably calculate the probability of success. Take a ship, for example. You have any number of factors that go into the success of the voyage—the experience of the captain, the likelihood of bad weather, the activity of pirates, the likelihood of smuggling, to name but a few. What I have found is that if one can gather about twenty-five variables on any given investment and calculate the odds of each variable, you arrive at a model for success that is robust."

"Twenty-five variables!" Darcy exclaimed. "A tedious business, is it not?"

"I find a strange enjoyment in it," Philips replied. "Some amuse themselves with a book. I find it excessively pleasant to sit down to a page of calculations."

"And in return for all the work, you likely take a percentage?"

"Twelve percent," Philips said with a nod. "Divided among the four of us."

"Not unreasonable. Can you make a profession of it?"

"I think we can. We have all built up a tidy sum over the years at university."

"If I could..." Darcy stopped to reflect. It would not do to be too forward here, but he liked what the fellow had to say. A small investment, a trial of sorts, could not be untoward? "I may be interested in what you do. Will you be setting up in London? Perhaps we might meet?"

"Oh no. No, I could not," Philips demurred. "I am honoured, sir, truly, but I would not wish to capitalise on the connexions of my cousin and her bridegroom. Forgive me if I spoke out of turn."

Darcy liked him even more for saying so. "I perceived nothing in your manner that seemed reaching. I asked you about it, if you recall. In any case, no promises, just a meeting. Would that do?"

Philips flushed a deep crimson and looked down. "I cannot tell you how much that means to me. I shall send my card to you when we are both in town, and if you should be inclined to take the meeting, I would be most grateful to you. If not, if upon further reflection you wish to refuse, then that is just as well."

"Not at all," Darcy replied firmly. "In fact, I insist upon it."

"And what does Mr Darcy insist upon?" Elizabeth had come to them from the side, unseen by Darcy. His heart leapt at the sound of her voice.

"Nothing to worry your pretty little head over, Lizzy," said Philips with a smirk. She replied by pinching him on the arm and scowling prettily.

It was then that Darcy perceived the source of familiarity in Philips's looks. His eyes, indeed, the entire shape of his countenance, were the more masculine version of Elizabeth's. He mentally shook his head, thinking it took no great feat of discernment there. They were, after all, cousins.

"Your mother is asking for you," Elizabeth informed her cousin. With a little frown of sympathy, she added, "I believe she is attempting to arrange lodgings for you with Mr Morris."

"Hey-ho! I had better get over there and stop her!" Philips turned and bowed to Darcy. "Thank you, sir, for your patient ear in hearing me rattle away."

"No, no, think nothing of that," Darcy said. "My pleasure entirely."

Philips left, but to Darcy's delight, Elizabeth did not follow him. She looked up at him, biting her lip.

"I hope my cousin was not importuning you in any way. He is very enthusiastic about his business prospects."

"I approached him," Darcy reassured her. "I find it a very interesting idea, in truth."

Elizabeth smiled, looking relieved. "I suppose it is. He has managed to amass a fortune of, oh, I think it must be two or three thousand by now, so—"

"Two or three thousand pounds?" Darcy exclaimed. "From...nothing?"

"I am not entirely certain where he began, but

knowing my aunt and uncle, I have to imagine it was all they could do for him just to send him to Oxford."

"Extraordinary." Darcy looked at the place where Philips had disappeared into the crowd. *Two or three thousand pounds on three percent of the returns? Surely she is mistaken?*

With her gaze also aimed towards the crowd, Elizabeth said, "I thank you for being so kind to him."

"It began as kindness," he said. "But if he has managed to build such a fortune from such small stakes, I think it will only redound to my benefit. I had already intended to meet him in town, and perhaps invest with him, but now I am positively determined."

"Really? You would meet him in town?"

The look of heartfelt delight that Elizabeth gave him took Darcy's breath away. "Is it so surprising? He evidently has a talent for making money, and in these uncertain times, he may well soon have a line outside of his door."

"He does have a talent," Elizabeth agreed, "but his connexions will always hinder him. Most men of better society will not speak to him."

"Stupid of them," Darcy remarked. "And stupid of me to have once been just like them. Thankfully, I have recently had occasion to see the error of my ways."

She looked at him quickly, then just as quickly dropped her gaze, her colour rising.

"Forgive me," Darcy said in a low voice. "I do not wish to make you uncomfortable."

She shook her head and said softly, "I am embarrassed by the things I said to you that night. I should have done better to hold my tongue."

"I do not agree. It seems I needed to hear those things, and who better than to hear it from than one I hold in such esteem."

After another quick peep at his face, she said, "I should think you would despise me."

"I was angry, at first," he admitted, "but my deep regard for you would not let it remain."

"Pray take heed, sir," she said with a light laugh. "Too much of that and I shall have to conclude that you have lost your resentful temper."

He smiled down at her. "Having a resentful temper is nothing to boast of, to be sure, and I should not have. But you must know by now which person I spoke of that day and what specific circumstances plagued me."

It took her a moment to recognise it. "Oh, you spoke of—"

With a quick glance about them, he said, "Wickham."

"I had not before considered," she said slowly, "how very recent those events must have been to the time when you were first here."

"'Twas the first week in September," he told her in low tones. "Georgiana had been there about a month."

Elizabeth looked up, her eyes searching his face, but what she might have said would be lost.

"Is not this cosy!" Miss Bingley exclaimed as she inserted herself into their tête-à-tête. "Miss Eliza, you are wanted by your dear mother. It seems a bridal emergency has arisen and only you can answer for the solution."

Both Darcy and Elizabeth looked over to where Mrs

Bennet was smiling and talking among a group of matrons. She did not seem to be in any way concerned for anything, wedding or otherwise, but Miss Bingley was determined. She had wound her arm through Elizabeth's and appeared willing to yank her from the space where she stood, by force if necessary. Elizabeth looked up at Darcy again and offered only the faintest smile before curtseying and asking him to excuse her.

CHAPTER THIRTEEN

W hen Darcy had arrived in Hertfordshire, he had been made aware of seven planned engagements. Two of them, the evening at the Robinsons' and the assembly, had been wasted by his own reticence. But the dinner at the Simpsons'? That one he had no idea about.

What he did know was that if there was to be an open door, it had opened last evening when he told Elizabeth he still held her in dear regard. Even that was not what he truly wished to say, which was that no matter what had gone between them, his love held true. That, he knew, he must show her.

Four events remained—a picnic, a ball, and a family dinner at Netherfield, and then the wedding and wedding breakfast. Beyond that, he had no expectation to remain in Hertfordshire.

"Four days to make her understand I love her and for her to have feeling enough to accept another proposal."

He nodded grimly at his reflection in the mirror, grateful Fields was not there to witness him talking to himself.

The servants, led by Mrs Nicholls and Miss Bingley, had set up the picnic just beyond the maze on a shady spot overlooking the winding countryside and, at some distance, the river. It was a lovely view, with the gently rolling countryside stretched out like a patchwork quilt, dotted with trees and the occasional stone cottage.

Darcy had arrived early, but many guests were already there. Alas, the guest he was most interested in was not, and so he paused briefly at a distance, pretending to admire the brightly coloured fabrics and paper lanterns that were hung from the trees and the sounds of the small group of musicians who were set up on one end.

He had been watching for the Bennets' carriage but Elizabeth appeared, suddenly, with only her eldest sister, and Darcy realised Bingley must have sent his carriage for them. The two ladies were descended upon immediately, the guests surging towards them to kiss Miss Bennet and hug Elizabeth and chatter happily about how soon the wedding was. Determined to join the group, he strode towards them, frowning when he saw his cousin approaching her as well. *Never mind him.*

He greeted the bride first and then turned to her sister. "Miss Elizabeth, how do you do," he said, bowing to her. Fitzwilliam, close beside him, echoed his salutations.

"Mr Darcy, Colonel." She smiled, sunshine and laughter in her eyes as she curtseyed.

"You are looking very lovely today." It was true. She wore a gown Darcy had never seen before—palest green with a sash of cornflower blue that matched the ribbons of her bonnet and the embroidery of her skirt.

"Only today, eh?" Fitzwilliam made a scolding sound with his tongue. "Ungenerous, Darcy. I say Miss Elizabeth is lovely every day."

"Happily, Miss Elizabeth is clever enough to comprehend that no slight was intended in my comment," Darcy replied evenly.

"Not this time, no. Now if we speak of last autumn, it is a different matter entirely!" Fitzwilliam chuckled and winked at her. Darcy was satisfied to see that she did not laugh in reply; indeed, she appeared rather mortified. It stoked Darcy's anger at his cousin.

"I have been, in the past, prodigiously uncivil, it is true, but Miss Elizabeth, I pray you take care. My cousin is an adept flatterer. Some might say he could charm the birds from the trees."

"So I can," Fitzwilliam agreed laughingly. "And Darcy here would then give them one of his infamous scowls and send them right back up."

Darcy remembered himself just in time to prevent a scowl that would have proved his cousin's point. "Miss Elizabeth, how well I do know of your fondness for nature and—"

"As do I!" the colonel interrupted. "How I have missed our walks in the groves of Rosings!"

"So you have said," Elizabeth remarked. Darcy wondered whether he heard a small note of irritation in her voice, or if that was merely wishful thinking.

"Are you fond of birds?" Darcy asked, then cursed

himself. Such a stupid question! "I mean, I am fond of birds. Some birds. Songbirds, or, um—"

"I have always admired your playing and singing." Fitzwilliam very nearly leered at her. "It puts the songbirds to shame."

For a moment, Elizabeth only stared at him, then glanced at Darcy. He was about to say something—though he knew not what that something was—when she dropped into a curtsey. "If you will both excuse me," she said and then, without waiting for anything more, left them.

"Well, that was all quite idiotic." Unseen by Darcy, Saye had arrived. "Really, men, telling her she's a bird? Short of allowing Florizel to hump her leg, I doubt there could be worse attempts at flirtation."

"Come. Now." Darcy gestured towards the edge of the maze nearby, a place where he could properly dress down his cousin without fear of being overheard. With a vexatious smirk on his countenance, Fitzwilliam did as ordered. Darcy followed him with Saye hard on their heels.

"What are you about, bringing up my insult?" Darcy rounded on Fitzwilliam as soon as he felt them concealed. "If you cannot win her by your own charms—"

"I do not think it unseemly to remind the lady which of us has been kind to her," his cousin replied loftily.

"Perhaps I should tell her how you are in a brothel every third night," Darcy spat.

"Perhaps I should tell her how well acquainted you are with your own handkerchiefs," Fitzwilliam retorted, stepping closer.

"Putting a handkerchief near that bump of yours would near suffocate the fellow," Darcy said, also taking a step forwards. "And we all know he has difficulty enough standing to attention."

"Take that back." Fitzwilliam gave Darcy a little shove.

"Why?" Darcy shoved back. "You cannot deny it, can you?"

"Stand down," Saye said, sounding irritated. He put one hand on his brother's chest, forcing him to step back, while he gave Darcy a look. The colonel shoved his hand away and, with a glare in Darcy's direction, cursed and then turned and stalked away.

"He is doing it up a bit too brown, do you not think?" Darcy asked.

"Perhaps he is," Saye replied, "but I would say you need to go browner. Have you truly never wooed a woman before?"

"I am doing everything I know to do." Darcy ran his hand through his hair.

"Then you must not know very much. Something as trite as telling her she is pretty sounds like her maiden aunt commending her for not showing too much bosom. It is better than insulting her, I shall grant you that, but scarcely."

"I said she was lovely, not pretty."

"Still stupid-sounding."

"I cannot arrange pretty compliments, Saye!"

"You can and you must. You are not amiable enough to think of things in the moment, so plan accordingly. Do not say 'you look lovely' say…" He thought briefly, then said, "Your beauty and grace have captivated my heart and my admiration of you is like nothing I have ever known before. Every inch of you is perfection and I am in awe of your beauty. You have an effortless way of moving that is so graceful and elegant, I am often left speechless in your presence."

With a smirk, he said, "So there, you have three. And if all else fails, think of a poem and tell her it seems as if it was written for her."

"It all sounds rather overdone, in my estimation."

Saye shrugged. "You had better think of something. Calling her Cousin Elizabeth will not be to your liking."

~

Elizabeth sat with a glass of lemonade in hand, listening to Jane and Bingley make love to one another. All three of them were seated on a blanket under a tree, with Elizabeth as far off the blanket as she could manage without risking grass stains on her skirt. Bingley and Jane occupied the corner farthest from her, nuzzling together, whispering, and laughing softly. She hardly supposed they needed a chaperon three days before the wedding, and in broad daylight no less, but in truth she was glad to sit and think.

She had turned it over in her mind again and again, what Mr Darcy had said the evening prior. *'I was angry, at first, but my deep regard for you would not let it remain.'* Was it possible that he loved her still? Could it be that the changes she saw in him truly were a result of what she had said? The idea that she, Elizabeth Bennet, had such a man as Mr Darcy in her power was astonishing. To imagine that he had altered something within himself for her? Even more astonishing.

Her eyes slipped towards Jane and Bingley and for a brief, mad moment, she imagined herself thus with Mr Darcy. Then she nearly laughed, the moment coinciding unfortunately with a sip of lemonade that made her sputter and spit. Happily, she recovered herself before anyone, even her companions, noticed.

Then again, I could probably choke to death before those two would notice, she mused, watching Bingley give Jane what appeared to be a kiss on the ear. *I do not believe Mr Darcy would act like that, not in full view of an entire party of people,* she decided. *But I do not know that I would either. We have that much in common at least; our more tender feelings are held close.*

Tender feelings for Mr Darcy. The very notion of that would have revolted her only a few weeks ago, but every time she spoke to him, everything they spoke about, revealed more of his good character. It had amazed her to learn he had first come into Hertfordshire, very likely heartsick with fear and sorrow for his own beloved sister, only a month after the near-disaster. Then to see Mr Wickham on the street! Such exemplary forbearance! She wondered that he had not thrown the man to the ground and pummelled him.

But it was not this which had occupied her thoughts since the night prior. She was lost in debating with herself whether he might still love her. At times it seemed impossible, but other times... She hardly knew what to think, particularly with the added complication of the colonel.

There was something amiss in Colonel Fitzwilliam's attentions to her. Looking out over the picnickers, she saw that he had joined the group playing quoits. He made a fine figure tossing the rings, but nevertheless he held no appeal for her. Over the last days, if she was honest, she had begun to dread seeing him approach. His behaviour did not strike her as genuine. It was why she had left him and Mr Darcy previously; his boldness was truly almost repulsive.

He had not been so in Kent, so why was he that way now? It defied sense, just like refusing to go and attend to land you had just inherited also defied sense. But she had no explanation for it, unless he merely wished to stymie his cousin? That seemed too cruel. Round and round she went, finding explanations and discarding them and never once arriving at a satisfactory answer.

Mr Darcy had left Lord Saye and was walking towards her. Her heart leapt at the look of determination upon his countenance as he came, and her chest seemed to somehow empty of air. She took a large swallow of her lemonade to calm herself as the truth she had been trying to set aside continued to prick at her consciousness. *As it happens, I just might wish to marry Mr Darcy after all. Quite ardently, in fact.*

"Miss Elizabeth," he said when he arrived at their party. His voice was a trifle too loud. Even Jane was startled from her love haze to look over at him.

He looked sheepish as he said, "I wonder if I might persuade you to take a walk?"

"A walk would be wonderful, thank you."

He looked pleased as he extended one arm to help her to her feet.

"I can only hope," she said conspiratorially, "that my two blanket-mates will not too long repine my absence."

They both glanced to where Jane and Bingley had resumed their lovemaking, and Mr Darcy chuckled. "I think they will shift along without you."

With no true direction, they set off, walking side by side. He asked whether she was having a pleasant day, and she assured him she was, then asked the same of him. They had not gone far before the colonel—who was beginning to remind Elizabeth of a horsefly—came trotting after them. "Where do you go, Darcy?"

Without looking at his cousin, Mr Darcy said, "Miss Elizabeth and I are taking a short walk."

"An excellent notion! I do not doubt Miss Elizabeth has any number of favourite paths she might show us."

Mr Darcy looked like he was clenching his jaw, but before he could speak, Elizabeth interceded, "I do, to be sure...but I am afraid I shall have to disappoint you, sir."

The colonel's grin dimmed very slightly. "Oh?"

"You see, I have just learnt of some important, um, wedding...things. Changes. And I must acquaint Mr Darcy with them at once." She smiled. "You will understand, I am sure. Perhaps later we might all play lawn bowls."

The colonel glanced between her and his cousin while Elizabeth willed him to move on. At last, he conceded. "That sounds excellent. I shall see you both in a bit, then." He turned on his heel and moved back towards the quoits game.

Elizabeth looked up at Mr Darcy, wondering what he thought of her boldness and surprised by her own unexpected wish be with him, and him alone.

"Shall we go into the garden?" Mr Darcy asked. "I understand some of the roses are beginning to bloom."

"By all means," she agreed.

CHAPTER FOURTEEN

"**E**veryone is in on it," Captain Carter explained to Lydia over lawn bowls. "And no one believes Darcy will get her."

Lydia snort-laughed. It was beyond diverting to imagine that Lizzy was the object of some great game amongst the gentlemen, a contest between Mr Darcy and his cousin! How droll! She wondered idly whom Lizzy would pick. Mr Darcy had more money, of course, but the colonel... She allowed her eyes to fall on that man. Yes, quite dashing.

"We sisters have our own little games, you know. For the sake of my own wager, I should dearly like to see her kiss Mr Darcy."

"The colonel is a favourite of most ladies who like a red coat," said Captain Carter, no doubt seeking reassurance of Lydia's favour. But she was determined not to give it to him. Men were too quick to become complacent. It did them good to feel uncertain.

"I can see that," she mused. "Not the handsomest

face, to be sure, but a lady does admire an athletic build like his."

The captain frowned and tossed his ball, which not only overshot the jack but sent it careering off. Lydia laughed loudly but quickly changed to a more placating countenance when he glanced her way.

"Bad luck!" she exclaimed. "I think the lawn is dreadful uneven, do not you?"

He looked relieved. "It is. What say you that we quit this stupid game and eat?"

"I should like that above all things," Lydia cooed, "but I do wonder…"

"What?"

"As much as I like a little wager among sisters, all I stand to gain for it is some old shoe roses."

"You are welcome to throw in with the regiment," Carter replied. "I can lay your bet for you, if you wish me to."

"I do," she said, lashes fluttering in a way she hoped was beguiling. "After all, more money in my pocket can only mean more fun in Brighton! Put it on Mr Darcy—I might as well have all my eggs in one basket."

They spoke more of Brighton as they went to where long tables had been laid with all manner of delicacies. Miss Bingley had done an excellent job arranging the picnic, commissioning cold meats and cheeses, heaps of fresh, crusty bread, a tower of delicious-looking fruits.

Lydia's father had also come to fill a plate, and hearing Carter rattling away about Brighton, he remarked in a very calm way, "We shall hope to have plenty of letters from you, young man, so that we too may know the delights of which you speak."

"I shall write to you, Papa," Lydia cried out staunchly. "Not every day, of course, but you may depend on a letter or two, that much I promise."

"About that... Finish your luncheon, child, and then I wish to speak to you."

❧

By all means. Lovelier words had never been spoken.

She just sent Fitzwilliam packing in favour of me. Darcy could scarcely credit that and yet, Fitzwilliam was banished and he alone had the privilege of extending his arm to receive Elizabeth's hand. *I think she did. She sent him packing.*

Her hand made a charming weight in the crook of his arm as they continued across the lawn towards the garden where the roses, as well as some spring blooms, made a beautiful prospect. *None so beautiful as the one beside me,* he thought.

A loud laugh made Elizabeth stiffen, then glance backwards to where one of her sisters played lawn bowls with Captain Carter. She gave a little frown and a sigh, followed with a shake of her head.

"I think you are very worried about your sister," Darcy observed mildly as they entered the garden.

"I was so very offended by the implication that my father did not do as he should to guide his daughters."

"I never should have presumed—"

"You were correct. Which makes it all the worse,

unfortunately." She laughed, but it sounded forced. "This scheme of hers to go to Brighton is excessively ill-advised. When I see how she behaves with my mother and father only paces away—"

"Elizabeth." He said her name in a low tone, and she stopped mid-stride to look up at him. "Pray worry no more about this."

"How can I not? Lydia is too heedless, far more concerned with entertaining herself than with ensuring that she—"

"Elizabeth." Darcy decided to risk covering her hand with his. "As it happens, I spoke to your father last night about this very thing. I told him why some men—one in particular—ought not to be trusted."

"Thank you." She gave him a smile, albeit a worried one. "Alas, my father is not the sort to hear gossip. Even with names and dates, he tends to disbelieve—"

"He believed me," Darcy said with quiet insistence. "For I gave him all the names and dates he required. Your father might be a sceptic, like his daughter, but I do think he had faith enough in my character to know I would not impugn my own sister so easily."

She came to a halt and turned towards him, her mouth agape. "You did not tell him—"

"I did."

"About...your sister?"

He nodded.

"Sir." She breathed the word, her eyes round and astonished. "I cannot believe—what made you do such a thing?"

"You," he said. "You alone. Yes, there is part of me

that is ashamed I had not done it before—countless other young women have undoubtedly fallen prey to him in consequence of my silence. But I acted for the sake of removing the worry from your heart. I could not allow you to suffer when I had the means to fix it."

Her cheeks flushed pink, and she looked at the ground; she was pleased, and he was pleased with himself for having occasioned her pleasure. *If you would marry me*, he told her silently, *I would see to it that you never had any cause to worry ever again.*

"I thank you," she said finally, "even if I know my sister will not. Who knows what might have happened to her there so far away from her family?"

"Perhaps nothing," he said, offering her his arm once more.

"Or perhaps everything," she concluded with a delicate shudder. "She is too poor to marry, but there is too much else to consider... But never mind any of that. She will be safe at Longbourn, thanks to you."

They rambled about the gardens for quite some time—Elizabeth hardly knew how long. She had never been overly fond of roses, but it seemed Mr Darcy's mother had been an enthusiast, and seeing Netherfield's roses provoked a great many memories within him.

"What is your favourite flower?" he asked her as they strolled towards the hedge maze.

"A flower I saw only once," she admitted. "And in a glass house no less—a camellia."

"A camellia? I do not think I have ever seen one. What did you like about it?"

"If I am being honest," she said with pursed lips, "it is entirely likely that I admire it just because it is unusual. Ask ten English ladies what flowers they like best and six will reply they like roses, another three will say lilies, and the last will surprise us with gardenia or orange blossom."

"So you will not be impressed by Pemberley's roses," he said in a musing tone. "Then I shall write, directly, to the head gardener and tell him to install as many camellias as he can."

She had no idea what to say to that. She stopped on the path and turned so that she was facing him with the questions of her heart looming large between them. "Camellias at Pemberley?"

He too stopped and turned towards her, speaking in an intimate tone. "Consider it my pledge to you. Whatever you wish for, if it is within my power to give it to you, then I shall. Large, small, everything in between. You would want for nothing, Elizabeth."

She looked down between them, still searching her mind for the best reply to what was almost another proposal.

"I do not mean to declare myself. Not yet, not in this way," he continued. "But if there is no hope, I pray you would tell me that. Do not leave me to deceive myself, I beg you."

Of its own accord, Elizabeth's hand rose, going to land upon the lapel of his jacket. He reached up immediately and covered it with his own hand and so they stood, suspended in a moment of great feeling. Her heart was throbbing painfully, so loud she was certain he could hear it. Her voice emerged just barely above a whisper as she said, "It is not hopeless."

His breath emerged in a sound between a groan and a sigh. He lifted their hands from his lapel, pressing a kiss onto her gloved palm.

It was easy then to rise on her toes, to angle her face in the direction that would be best to receive his kiss. His eyes widened and seemed to question her—but then he closed them, all the better, it seemed, for his lips to claim hers.

His lips were soft and shockingly warm, but she had little time to think anything of that before a strident voice rang out.

"You! How *dare* you!"

CHAPTER FIFTEEN

A cold dash of icy fear immediately recalled Elizabeth to sensibility. She leapt backwards from Mr Darcy, then turned to see her youngest sister standing at some distance away from them on the path. Lydia's face was nearly purple with rage as she advanced towards them, glaring at Mr Darcy.

"You!" she shrieked again.

"Lydia." Elizabeth hastened to intervene, thinking how odd it was to have Lydia, of all people, concerned for a stolen kiss among the hedges. "It is not what it seems, and if you will come with me—"

Lydia pushed by her, very nearly flying at Mr Darcy with skirts and ribbon and violent indignation swirling about her. "Hateful, odious man!"

"Lydia, stop!" Elizabeth cried just as Mr Darcy, in very sedate accents, said, "Do not be dismayed, Miss Lydia."

"Not dismayed? You have ruined everything!" A sob choked Lydia's last words, and Elizabeth observed tears in her sister's eyes when she turned towards her. "Mr Darcy thinks that since he is such a dullard, he ought to prevent others from having fun too! My entire summer is ruined!"

This is about Brighton, Elizabeth recognised with relief. *Not the fact that she saw me kissing Mr Darcy.* She took her sister's arm and tried to pull her away. "Lydia, dearest, come with me."

Lydia wrenched her arm out of Elizabeth's grasp. "Horrible, odious man!" She made a motion as though she intended to shove Mr Darcy with both hands; fortunately, she was too far away from him to make contact. It only frustrated her more, and she stamped her foot. "He told Papa that he should not let me go to Brighton!"

"There are dangers, real dangers, that a young lady of gentle birth might meet with in such a place," Mr Darcy said to her. "It is difficult, I know, to be of an age where—"

"Yes, a real danger of someone having a laugh or two instead of being stuck in this dreadful town where nothing ever happens to anyone! Mrs Forster is going to watch over me!" Lydia shouted.

"I have lately learnt that Mrs Forster is with child," Mr Darcy continued in that same calm, steady tone. "She will have enough to occupy her without going round to balls and parties all the time."

Alas, it held too much reason for Lydia. She uttered a wordless growl of frustration, and then resorted to her long-cherished response to anything that vexed her. "I hate you! You are the most vile man I ever knew!"

"Lydia!" Elizabeth said immediately. She shot Mr

Darcy a contrite look, then turned to her sister and said, "Apologise to Mr Darcy *now* for this behaviour."

"Why should I? And why should you want me to? You hate him as much as anyone, Lizzy, and you would hate him even more if you knew what he was about!"

What he was about? Fortunately, Elizabeth did not need to wait long for Lydia to explain. Her sister raised her chin, eyes glittering meanly at Mr Darcy while she announced, "'Tis all a bet. All these grand gentlemen in London have made bets on you, to see whether you will marry him or his cousin." With a little sniff, she looked over her shoulder in the general direction of the party. "Obviously take the colonel. At least he knows what it is to smile and have a laugh now and then."

Elizabeth looked to Mr Darcy, standing just where she had kissed him only minutes earlier. He dropped his eyes to the pebbled path, saying nothing as she begged him silently to laugh or declare it all nonsense. But he did not.

"That is not true, Lydia," she said, hearing her uncertainty revealed in the tone of her voice. "It cannot be."

Mr Darcy said nothing.

"Yes, it *is* true. All sorts of bets, from what dear Wickham has told me," Lydia announced. "Thousands of pounds, Lizzy. *Thousands*."

"Sir?" Elizabeth said, unable to look at the silent form of the man she had only just begun to love. "Is this true?"

He swallowed visibly and said what were, to Elizabeth's mind, the worst words that he could possibly say. "I can explain."

❧

Amid bewildered distress, Elizabeth found herself bolting into the maze, abandoning Mr Darcy to Lydia. She no longer cared whether her sister insulted him or called him names; if Lydia kicked him square in the shins, it would be no less than he deserved. Hot tears blinded her and obscured her progress.

I can explain. No one could explain such an insult as this. He had made her ridiculous, and that she could not abide. Was that what all this was about? Some wager? Some sort of revenge against her, to humiliate her before everyone in both London and Meryton?

You need explain nothing, she had hissed in reply. *You are just as I ever thought you were—arrogant, disdainful of the feelings of others—and now I may add that you are heinously manipulative as well. I was a fool to imagine you could be amiable, or good—but you are an excellent actor, I shall grant you that.*

She careered about, twisting, turning, and weeping. *I am an object of scorn and derision and wagers and silliness, an object, not a lady of worth.* She was a fool to imagine Mr Darcy had changed. *She* had changed, yes, she had softened towards him, believed that he might be someone she could truly admire, but it turned out she was a fool. *A leopard cannot change its spots, and neither can a Darcy, apparently.*

And the colonel! He had behaved so oddly throughout, he must have served some purpose to the scheme, some sort of challenge or a test to her. She could not work out his exact purpose, but she had known something nefarious was afoot in his attentions.

At length she came to the centre of the maze and

paused, swiping away the tears on her cheeks and in her eyes. She took several deep breaths and looked about her. She had not intended to come so far; Netherfield's maze was known throughout the county for being large and complex, built to emulate that in Hampton Court Palace, though Elizabeth knew not how near to the mark it came. To add to that, it was overgrown and thus to extricate herself from it would require more effort than she had wished to expend.

"And I have somehow lost my bonnet," she said ruefully, hoping rather than believing she might be able to retrace her steps and find it.

She trudged through the maze for quite some time, the twists and turns seeming alternately familiar and not. At last, feeling chilled and tired, she chose to shove through the hedge to escape, no longer caring about her appearance or her dignity. Why should she when Mr Darcy had made her a laughingstock? Might as well sink into the figure of ridicule he had made her.

The party had mostly broken up when at last she approached the clearing where it had been set up. The little orchestra was gone, and the servants were bustling about folding blankets, carrying the uneaten food back to the kitchen, and helping the remaining few guests finish their merriment. She saw none of her family and wondered, briefly, if they had simply decamped, sparing her no thought. Another tear leaked out at that self-pitying thought, and it almost made her laugh at herself.

A figure had approached her from one side but she paid him no mind until he said, "Miss Bennet. Well. This is a sight."

At least it is not Mr Darcy or the colonel, she thought with relief. *Only Lord Saye.* "Excuse me, my lord."

"What have you been doing?" he asked, his handsome face looking horrified. "There are *sticks* in your hair."

She raised one hand, feeling the leaves and small branches entwined in among her curls. "Yes, well, I…um, I got a bit turned about in the maze and decided to go through rather than find my way out."

"And that made you cry?"

"No, no, it was…" She dropped her hand and shook her head. "Nothing. Nothing at all. If you will excuse me, sir."

She curtseyed and nearly walked off but stopped herself, hoping that the suddenness of her enquiry would cause him to be forthcoming. "Do *you* have money on this?"

He tilted his head, a benign smile on his lips like the very picture of innocence. "On what?"

She gave him what she hoped was a withering look. "On *me*. And whether I might marry Mr Darcy or…or your brother."

"Oh!" He grinned at her, perfectly unrepentant. "Yes, I do. Care to give me any hints as to your inclination?"

The easiness of his admission took her aback. "I despise them both, if you would know. I have already told Mr Darcy he is the last man in the world I would ever marry—"

"Ouch!" his lordship interjected cheerfully.

"—and now your brother may join him there."

"Why?" He leant on his walking stick. "What have you against Richard?"

"Because he is a part of this," she said, her anger beginning to stoke itself again. "I could not make him out—he was so determined to put me off in Kent, and *that* was awkward enough—but then to come here and behave in such a…a peculiar fashion! Even more awkward. I hardly knew whether I should be seduced or stupefied."

"Seduced or stupefied! Miss Elizabeth, you are brilliant." Lord Saye chuckled. "I cannot wait to tease him with that. He thinks himself such a favourite of the ladies."

"Perhaps you will gratify my brilliance by helping me understand this scheme. Was it all some farce that would have ended with a broken engagement? The derision of my neighbours? *None* of it was in earnest, that much is certain," she declared, feeling righteous indignation surging through her.

Lord Saye seemed almost puzzled by her stance. "Why do you think so?"

"Because…" Elizabeth paused, drawing in a calming breath. "Because it was all so strange. The colonel was entirely different than he was in Kent. He came here with some tale of an estate that he seemingly cannot be bothered to go and look at. And you tell me—if this place is so near to Matlock, how has he gone thirty years without ever seeing it? When your own relation lived there? I hardly knew what to make of such a tale, or of the fact that he seems to be able to make his eyes twinkle on command."

Lord Saye coughed in a way that sounded like a laugh but said nothing.

"And then to discover all the wagers? So humiliating! I shall be the laughingstock of London Society!"

"Humiliating? Hardly," he scoffed. "Do you have any idea what is the worst fate that can befall a young woman in London?"

"Ruination?"

"Not even close."

She sighed, heavily and theatrically. "What then?"

"Oblivion. The greatest fear of anyone who arrives on the doorstep of Society is that no one knows your name or worse—that no one cares. It is excessively difficult to raise the interest of people whose first object is world-weariness, and who are surrounded by wealthy, beautiful, witty people all the time." He pointed at her. "Your name is already on everyone's lips. Everyone who is anyone is awaiting your choice with bated breath and they are mad to meet you."

"That cannot be true."

"But it is. The only person who really stands to lose face here is, well, the loser."

Elizabeth raised her eyes to the heavens again. His assurances were assuaging her anger, and she hated that. "But my reputation, my dignity—"

"Are untouched." Lord Saye shrugged. "My dear girl, the betting books in the gentlemen's clubs are absolutely *filled* with wagers of all kinds. This one is only made more interesting because of the persons involved. Darcy does not make a habit of being a part of this sort of thing. He has never been much of a gambler."

Now it was her turn to give a haughty sniff. "No

doubt Mr Darcy stands to gain a great deal of money in all this."

"Darcy stands to gain nothing. He did not bet. Too unsure of his own success, poor sod, no matter how much he tried to bluster at my brother. Why do you think we... Well, no. That is a story for another time."

"Why do I think you—what? That sounds like the very bit I should know."

"You have told me why you doubt my brother," he said smoothly, ignoring her, "but why Darcy?"

"Because a man does not change his character," she said firmly. A small prick from her conscience reminded her of her recent revelations to herself—that she had not *understood* his character, but she ignored it.

"Perhaps not his character, but he may change his customs," Lord Saye replied. "Darcy will always be given to some amount of pride, perhaps some tendency to self-centredness—but we all have our defects. It is the desire to overcome them that is truly remarkable, and *that* he is most certainly wanting to do. For you."

"If you mean to tell me that Mr Darcy came here with an earnest wish of winning my hand, then I shall say..." She trailed off, reason suddenly asserting itself. Anger at being tricked, blind anger, had overtaken her, so much so that she had not really thought about Mr Darcy's motives in all of this. Did she actually have reason to suspect it was his doing? It was not his sort of thing, not by half. Anger left her in a sickening rush, leaving dismay in its wake.

"He loves you and you love him," Lord Saye

informed her. "Pray do not shake your head. I know I am right."

"What makes you think I am in love with Mr Darcy?"

Lord Saye frowned in thought but at length said, "Miss Bennet, you look untidy, and I prefer women with blonde hair. Moreover, I think your sisters are too young to be out."

She drew back, nose and brow wrinkled. "Thank you. I am sure I am well-pleased to take your strictures under advisement," she said sarcastically.

"Does that injure you? That I should think so?" He seemed strangely enthusiastic at the prospect.

"No. Perhaps vexed me a little."

"Did it injure you when my aunt was insufferable with *her* opinions? That had to cause some embarrassment. Richard said she was positively ghastly, even for her."

"I did not enjoy it but no, it did not injure me."

"Ha! See there!" He clapped and then pointed at her gleefully. "Thank you—my point is proved!"

"What point is that?"

"Darcy's opinions were more powerful because you cared what he thought." Lord Saye leant back, a satisfied smirk on his face and one hand on his hip. "If you did not have some feeling towards him, you would have felt just as you did when I insulted you. By the bye, I think you very pretty, perhaps even beautiful, when you are not out thrusting yourself through hedges."

"You are a madman," she said with a weak laugh.

"You would not be the first lady to say so," he agreed

amiably. "But here is the material point. There is a game afoot, it is true, but it is not Darcy's game."

"But—"

"I assure you, he disliked it heartily. He would not involve himself in such a thing for money and certainly not for revenge. No, there is but one thing that would induce him to participate in such an escapade, and I daresay we all know what that is."

Love. Elizabeth dared not say it aloud, for suddenly she felt like crying, laughing, or perhaps vomiting. *I did it again.* She had, once again, gone off into a fury at Mr Darcy, believing the worst and knowing the least. Again, she had been blind, prejudiced, partial, and absurd. Again, she had thought the worst of him. Again, she had spoken in anger, her tongue unbridled and fierce. If anyone's character was unchangeable, it was hers.

"He really—" she said in a voice that emerged hoarse. She paused and cleared her throat. "He truly had no hand in the wagers?"

"It began between himself and Richard and, if I am honest, Richard rather goaded him into it. Said he could have you a million times over before you would ever look at Darcy."

"That was excessively cruel."

"But *necessary.* Pray do not think Richard undertook it lightly. Darcy was on the verge of leaving to go and propose to our cousin, such was his despair. We had to stop him."

"Propose to Miss de Bourgh?" Elizabeth exclaimed, but Lord Saye kept talking over her, speaking quickly. *He does not wish me to stop and think about the fact that the colonel was being purposely goading, purposely cruel to Darcy. Why?*

"Events thereafter spun beyond his control. Darcy had commissioned a carriage, and Richard said if he won, it was his, and then Alfie Hurst showed up and my friend Sir Frederick, who never looks away from a chance for easy money. Gentlemen do love to gamble—as do your own sisters, I might add."

"My sisters?"

"I was passing by that youngest one with Captain Carter earlier. Evidently there are some shoe roses up for grabs if someone can make you kiss Darcy."

Which I did! And now he will absolutely, positively despise me. There is no return from such as this. Once was a mistake. A second time is an unredeemable shade in my character.

"Now if you will excuse me, I must be off. Racing about the countryside myself in a manner most indecorous, if you must know. What you women do to us all!" He touched the brim of his hat and sauntered off.

CHAPTER SIXTEEN

Darcy had been thirteen years old the first time he was thrown from a horse, but he still recalled the suddenness of it, the way his mind had struggled to comprehend the jarring thud, and to understand why he was suddenly on his back staring at the sky. Pain had been suspended for such a time as to make him think he had escaped it—until he realised that no, he had not, as it came roaring up to find him.

It was the same sensation to be left in the company of Lydia Bennet, the taste of Elizabeth's kiss still on his lips and her angry words ringing in his ears. The disappointment was almost too much to be borne.

"I shall never forgive you," Miss Lydia said, her petulance unabated.

"I would never forgive myself if something happened to *you*," he retorted. Disappointment made him wish to lash out at the silly girl. "You may think that at fifteen—"

"I am sixteen next week!"

He managed to not roll his eyes but spoke with all the

impatience that was warranted. "Miss Lydia, I am going to be perfectly frank with you. A girl of your age who has been properly protected by her family has no idea of the baser instincts of men—particularly men ensconced in the company of other men for an extended time. By the time you understood it, you would have been too much damaged by it to ever recover the life you ought to have had."

"I only want to have some fun!" She looked like she wanted to stamp her foot again but did not. "Nothing would have happened to me!"

"Do you think any lady who finds herself ruined or injured set out planning for it?" Darcy shook his head. "Believe me when I say I have *known* young ladies, your very age, who have gone out on a lark and come back forever changed. I would much rather have you hate me than suffer a similar fate. No, we can never know what might have happened, but I can only urge you this: do not be in such a hurry to grow up. Enjoy your girlhood."

She sighed, frustrated and pouty. "You simply have no idea, Mr Darcy, how it is to live in such a place as this! How would you like it if a once-a-month assembly was the only thing you ever had to look forward to?"

"I would not like it at all," he said. He thought a moment, then added, "How is this? I hope to persuade your sister to marry me, and if I can, you may come and stay with us in London for as long as you wish."

"That sounds like a grand plan," Miss Lydia replied with no little sarcasm, "save for the fact that Lizzy is as likely to marry you as she is to sprout wings and fly."

With that she flounced off.

At least it does not seem that she saw us kissing, Darcy thought grimly. *Surely she would have said something about that.*

He walked a short way into the maze. Netherfield's maze was famed for being uniquely vast and complex— almost a labyrinth. It also had innumerable twists and turns and four points of exit, so he knew, reasonably, that he had little chance of finding Elizabeth if she did not wish to be found. It was nearly a ten-minute walk to the centre, and he did that, finding her bonnet but otherwise no evidence of her.

What to do, what to do? he thought as he slowly walked back towards the house. *What I shall not do is take this one on the chin. This does not end here, not at the hands of Lydia Bennet. Tomorrow,* he decided. *I shall find her tomorrow at the ball, when emotions have subsided, explain it all as best as I can, and then hope for the best.*

If he was not engaged by tomorrow evening, he decided, then he would die trying.

When Lord Saye left her, Elizabeth continued towards the clearing. She looked about in the vain hope that she might see Mr Darcy, but she saw no one save her father, standing and chatting with the elder Mr Goulding under a tree. *I suppose they did not abandon me after all.* Just another thing she had been wrong about.

She walked towards the pair slowly, wishing with every step that she might catch a glimpse of Mr Darcy, or hear him call out her name. Her wishes went unanswered. When she arrived, her father informed her that he had sent her mother and sisters on without her, and that Mr Goulding would return them to Longbourn in his carriage.

The night was long while Elizabeth considered what she had, *again*, done. No matter how she twisted and turned it in her head, she could not find any way to absolve herself. *The errors of my ways*, she thought grimly, *are evidently unshakeable.* The worst of it was that she would be required to see Mr Darcy on several more occasions, most notably the wedding itself. She knew not how she would survive any of it; how to look at the man she had just kissed, the man with whom she had been falling in love, and be met with anger. No, worse than anger—coldness. *He came here in hopes of winning my hand, and I have treated him abominably.*

The morning came too soon. Elizabeth was yet lying abed when she heard her mother exclaiming in the rooms beneath. She wondered what was happening as she heard a great deal of activity, followed by the sound of someone rushing up the stairs. Moments later, Jane burst into their shared bedchamber.

"It is here," she said, her face aglow. "Finally, my wedding gown is here! My mother is hard on my heels with it."

The gowns that Elizabeth, Jane, and Mrs Bennet had commissioned in London had been unforgivably delayed. Mrs Gardiner had gone herself to the shop and impressed upon the lady how very unlikely it was that she would receive more orders from the newly married and wealthy

Mrs Bingley if the very gown she was to marry in was not delivered on time. But it seemed they were, at last, at Longbourn, even if it was with barely two days to spare.

"Thank goodness," Elizabeth said, getting herself out of bed.

"Oh, if this dressmaker even knew what she has done to my nerves!" Mrs Bennet exclaimed as she entered the room, Hill and Sarah behind her bearing the parcels. Hill set hers down and bustled off but Sarah stayed to help them dress.

"There, there, Mama," Elizabeth said. "I am sure they are done to perfection."

Alas, relief was short lived. The gown removed from its packing was rather unlike that which Jane had commissioned. What her sister had wished for was a satin gown in palest blush pink, with light trim on the skirt, with fuller sleeves tucked up to allow rosettes made of the same pink satin to peek through. Mrs Bennet had protested, violently, at the lack of lace on the gown, but Jane had held firm and had at last prevailed—or so she had believed. Evidently Mrs Bennet had gone back to the dressmaker, and the dressmaker had complied with a full lace overdress as well as even more lace coming down from the sleeves to cover the elbows. Tears welled up in Jane's eyes the moment she saw it, but she blinked them back, saying nothing.

Mrs Bennet was delighted by it, too much so to even notice Jane's quiet. "You see! I told you it needed just a touch of lace! You will be the very picture of elegance, my darling girl! Bingley will be too astonished to speak!"

Jane said not a syllable as she was dressed in the

gown—which, Elizabeth noted, seemed to have also become significantly more low cut in the bodice—and remained silent and still in front of the cheval mirror as her mother and Sarah tugged at the lace and exclaimed over her beauty.

"I do not think you have ever been more beautiful," Mrs Bennet enthused. "Is she not beautiful? Lizzy, say something to your sister."

That Jane was deeply distressed was perfectly obvious to Elizabeth, but she dutifully told her how beautiful she looked. Jane offered a wan smile and submitted meekly to the removal of the garment, which was hung on the door of their closet. After one last sigh of happy satisfaction, Mrs Bennet and the maid left the two sisters alone, with instructions that Elizabeth should try hers on as well.

Jane immediately turned to her sister, her blue eyes brimming with tears.

"It is a beautiful gown," Elizabeth said immediately and desperately. "You look so lovely in it."

"I hate it!" Jane said with a little choked sob, and then the tears began in earnest. She sank onto her bed, one hand covering her face as she wept.

Elizabeth hastened to sit beside her, putting a hand on her back and feeling her sister's shoulders shake with her sobs.

"It is so ugly. It is nothing at all like I wished it to be! What did she do, buy every bolt of lace in London? And ecru lace no less? Ugly! It looks like one of her handkerchiefs!"

Elizabeth rubbed her sister's back in small circles. "She likely believed it was less elegant without lace."

"Well, I think it is less elegant with the lace, and very matronly," Jane replied, then gave a hiccoughing little sob. "You must think me dreadfully ungrateful. It must have been such an expense to her but...but..."

"But an expense you never asked for, nor wished for," Elizabeth consoled. "No one could have real gratitude for such an imposition. This was your wedding gown, not hers."

"I cannot believe it. It is so ugly, so very unlike what I wanted to look like on my wedding day." Jane sighed, wiping the tears from her eyes. "I cannot bear imagining it. My only consolation is that I cannot look at myself."

That made Elizabeth chuckle a little. "Jane, it takes more than mere lace to overwhelm your beauty. Bingley will be so busy staring into your eyes, he will not give the gown a second look."

"You can be certain Caroline and Louisa will have much to say about it, and none of it good."

Elizabeth, alas, could not disagree with that.

"How does yours look?" Jane asked. "Did she put lace on that too?"

"I confess, I have not even looked at it yet." The other dress box had been brought to their bedchamber as well but rested unopened on Elizabeth's bed. She opened it now, revealing the very gown that she had expected to see. The sleeves resembled Jane's with the small cascade of puffs but had neither the rosettes nor the terrible lace. "Only the bride was treated to such an overabundance, it seems."

Jane looked utterly defeated, her mouth downturned and her shoulders bent as she reached out one hand to lightly touch her sister's gown. She gave a little sniff. "It is very elegant. You will look beautiful in it."

"Or perhaps you will."

Her sister gave a little laugh, clearly not understanding.

Elizabeth sat down next to her. "Would you prefer to wear this gown?"

Jane paused in caressing the gown and looked at her.

"We could take the rosettes off yours and put them in the sleeves, and it would be very near the gown you wished for, just ivory instead of pink."

"Can one marry in ivory?"

"Why not?"

Jane gently fingered the gauze overdress, which had been delicately ornamented with little seed pearls. "I am taller than you," she said finally, a weak protest.

"Barely," Elizabeth replied. "And in any case, I was wearing a small heel when I had it fitted. I venture it will be just right for you."

"The bodice, though?"

"Could be easily let out."

"But then what would you wear?" Both sisters' gazes turned to the lace monstrosity hanging on the door. Understanding dawned on Jane immediately. "No, I could not ask you to do that. You dislike such an abundance of lace as much as I do, and the ecru—"

"Makes us both look pallid. But it is not my wedding day," Elizabeth replied. "And you have not asked anything of me. I am offering it. Come, let us try them on and see how it would look."

Not so many minutes later, the two sisters stood attired in the opposite gowns they were meant to have. Elizabeth knew immediately she had done well; Jane's eyes finally looked happy as she beheld herself in the ivory gown—which did not yet fasten at the back but would be easily altered. For herself, the pink concoction was too much adorned to really suit her, but for one morning, a morning of such importance to Jane, it would do.

But Mr Darcy will see you in this gown. Elizabeth quashed that thought immediately. Once again, she had misunderstood him and been cruel to him; once again, he had been driven away by her tongue. It seemed that they had no talent for being in accord; a few days in company was bound to end in some misunderstanding or another. An excess of lace was nothing to the excess of cruelty she routinely gave him.

"But who can do all of this letting out and hemming in?" Jane asked. "The entire house is upside down getting ready for this breakfast, our sisters' gowns are yet being finished by Sarah, our mother is not going to want—"

"Me." Elizabeth put a hand on her arm. "I can do it. I shall do it."

Although she did not like to admit it, Elizabeth was far more skilled with a needle than anyone ever thought she could be. She attributed it to one winter of illness when she had been set abed with dreadful colds four times complete. Much as she enjoyed reading, too many days of doing nothing else would have sent her mad, and so she had honed her sewing skills.

"When?" Jane asked. "The ball is tonight, then tomorrow is the dinner, and we shall scarcely have a moment to rest. Mama will not hear of you remaining home for any of it."

Elizabeth knew she was correct. Much as she would have loved to miss the ball, it was not possible. But it *was* possible to be at Netherfield and not at the ball.

"We shall send it over to Netherfield," she told Jane. "Then, once I have had a dance or two, I shall slip below stairs and work down there. You know Mrs Nicholls will allow me to sit in a corner somewhere."

"Oh no, I could not ask you to do that."

Elizabeth removed her arms from the pink gown and began to slide it off down her body. "It will be a relief to be able to absent myself from the dancing."

"Why?" Jane eyed her curiously. "The colonel has seemed very friendly with you."

Elizabeth had not confided in her sister about the wagers, or her reaction to learning of them, thinking there was no cause to put a damper on her sister's felicity. Now, she kept her attention ostensibly on the gown, picking it up off the floor, shaking it, laying it carefully on the bed.

"Mr Darcy has as well."

"Let us hope Mama has not noticed, else she will be determined that I should marry one, or both of them," Elizabeth said, gesturing to Jane to turn so that she could help her remove her gown.

"But surely you wish to—"

"What I wish is for my sister to be happy on her wedding day." She set to work undoing what buttons had been fastened on the ivory gown. "It is all decided! Nothing more to be said, or done, save for trusting me to make the changes."

"Will not our mother be very angry about this?"

"If she is," Elizabeth said, sliding the gown away from Jane's body, "then we shall remind her that no one wished for all this lace! You are three-and-twenty, Jane, she cannot dress you up as if you were a child and had no say in the matter."

Turning, Jane threw her arms around her sister. She kissed her on the cheek, and said, "You are the dearest sister in the world."

CHAPTER SEVENTEEN

T he ball truly was a compliment to Jane. *Miss Bingley has done well*, Elizabeth thought, taking in the flowers, the candles, and the chalk on the dance floor that was a special design incorporating Jane and Bingley's initials entwined with vines.

Some part of her was excessively conscious of the two men she wished most to avoid. She walked about a little, dreading any meeting, but fortune was kind. She saw neither of them, though she did see Lord Saye with a shockingly pretty young woman with whom Elizabeth was not acquainted. The elusive Miss Goddard, perhaps?

She crossed paths with them not long thereafter, as the set began to form. An introduction to Miss Goddard revealed her to be as sweet as she was pretty, and Lord Saye to be plainly smitten with her. Elizabeth smiled at that, wondering at how uncomplicated romance was for some people.

"Miss Elizabeth, you are the talk of London," Miss Goddard told her.

"So I hear." Elizabeth decided to treat it humorously and rolled her eyes at the pronouncement.

"There have been bets on my engagement—or lack thereof—for some years now," Miss Goddard confided.

"Bets which I intend to bring to a conclusion very soon," Lord Saye interjected.

"I have already told you I am not going to marry you," she said to him but smiled in such a way that it seemed more encouraging than not.

"We shall see about that," Lord Saye replied airily. "I have some arts remaining which are yet unknown to you."

With that, Miss Goddard gave Elizabeth a roll of her eyes and a mouthed 'help me' but it all seemed in good humour and she allowed Lord Saye to lead her off soon after.

When the dance began, Elizabeth still had not seen either Colonel Fitzwilliam or Mr Darcy, and she was heartily thankful for that. She danced with Philips, making sure that her mother saw them. Afterwards, relieved to escape, she hurried below stairs to play seamstress for the rest of the night.

Mrs Nicholls had a little room near the kitchen that had a long table and little stools that were ideal for sewing. She seemed scandalised that Elizabeth was missing the ball to sew, saying to her, "Miss Bingley's maid could surely be put to work?"—but Elizabeth refused her, saying Miss Bingley's maid was likely collapsed in exhaustion after tending to her mistress. That made the housekeeper laugh.

"I am not inclined to dance tonight," Elizabeth reassured her. "I was quite looking forward to my evening below stairs."

Mrs Nicholls fussed a bit more, lighting lamps and bringing in a glass of ratafia for Elizabeth to sip while she worked. Soon enough, however, Elizabeth was alone with the gowns, and it suited her very well. Or at least she *told* herself it suited her. She wondered how different things might have been if Lydia had not said what she said, or if she herself had not lost her temper as she had. "Or if pigs flew and my eyes were blue," she said with a little chuckle. What was the point in regretting what could not be?

Fixing the pink gown to fit her was easy enough. She easily took in the bodice, and equally rapidly took up the hem. Before half an hour had passed, it was done. She inspected her handiwork, satisfied with what she saw, though she shuddered anew at the excessive ornamentation. "How is it that there seems to be even more lace on this? Is it multiplying, or expanding in some way?" she wondered aloud.

For Jane's gown, more work was required. Elizabeth first let out the bodice, relying on her knowledge of her sister to guide her; there would be time for more minor alterations tomorrow, she hoped. Then she began the more arduous task of removing the rosettes from the pink gown and inserting them into the sleeves of the ivory. She had just begun on the second when a noise from outside the little room startled her. Her heart plunged when she looked up and beheld Mr Darcy on the threshold, gazing at her.

"May I join you?"

Not trusting herself to speak, she nodded, and he stepped into the room. She heard a thud as the door swung closed behind him.

"Oh," he said, turning, "I suppose I should—"

"It does not signify," she said. "The servants are busy with the ball." She could not imagine that Mr Darcy would speak to her for more than a few minutes.

She studied the gown intently as he settled himself on the stool beside hers. Her hands had begun to shake, so she kept them hidden beneath the folds of material, though to continue sewing was impossible.

"What are you doing down here?" he asked in a voice much gentler than she deserved.

"Jane's gown—" Her voice betrayed her, breaking on the word 'gown'. Suddenly tears swam in her eyes, making everything a blur. She did not dare look up and prayed, mightily, that he would leave her.

She could not speak, and it seemed Mr Darcy would not either. Was he so content to merely sit and watch her staring at Jane's wedding gown? What did he want? An apology? Very well; she would apologise. With a deep breath, she raised her eyes to look at him. He perched uncomfortably on the stool, his long legs clad in ballroom finery. He wore a dark blue jacket—she had never seen him in that colour, and it suited him well.

"Sir, I-I spoke to your cousin—"

"Which?"

"Lord Saye."

"Pray disregard whatever he said," Mr Darcy said immediately. "He is a rattle and enjoys being shocking."

She smiled faintly. "He explained the particulars of the wagers to me. How it all happened."

"You must believe me when I tell you I care nothing for any bet," he replied fiercely. "You must know enough of me to know that money could never induce me to chase a woman who had spurned me."

"So he told me."

That took a bit of the starch out of him. "He did?"

"My immediate thought was to imagine it was all a joke at my expense, some little farce whereby you would pretend—"

"I would never do that," he interrupted. "Never."

"I know. Once again, Mr Darcy, I have misjudged you. I do not expect your forgiveness—"

"You have it." He swallowed hard. "And I pray you will find it in your heart to forgive me for all this nonsense. I was not the originator of it, and all I stood to lose was the right to give you a carriage, but I ought to have done more to stop them."

"Lord Saye mentioned the carriage. I assumed he spoke in jest or was exaggerating."

"He often does, but not this time." He sighed, shifting on the stool. "You will recall the night you dined at Rosings, when you played the pianoforte with Fitzwilliam turning pages for you. I came and stood over you. You teased me about practising—said you would be proficient but you had not taken the trouble to practise and that I was a man of the world and ought to have practised speaking to you."

He shook his head with a regretful smile on his lips. "I perceived that you were perhaps playing coy with me, or in some way signalling...interest."

"I see," she said. He would not be the first man misled by her lively spirits, but that he should be susceptible to them was surprising.

"I...I am an arrogant fool and thought it was only a matter of time until I had your hand. I believed it was up to me, that once I had reconciled myself to offering for you, it would be done."

Elizabeth felt herself colour as he spoke those words. To cover her consternation, she reached for another rosette and resumed her sewing.

"So I wrote, that very night, to Hatchett & Co, telling them I intended to commission a new town coach. I also..."—he drew a deep breath—"I also opened accounts with some of the...the warehouses in town, thinking you might wish to...to redecorate the houses."

"Redecorate your houses!"

"If we were engaged, they would be our houses," he said quietly.

Our houses. A glance revealed a tenderness in his eyes that she had not before seen. It was somehow incredibly endearing, the manner in which he said it. *He truly wanted me as his wife,* she thought, and it was a notion more shocking than it ought to have been. *He was imagining our future life together, wishing me to have all the honour of being Mrs Darcy.*

She had not before considered how amazing it was that Mr Darcy had wished to share with her all that he had: his houses, his fortune, his name...his future.

"My house in town"—he continued to speak, to explain to her his plans and preparations—"is very dark. My mother did it up in wood panelling and heavy drapery, as was in fashion at the time of her marriage, but I could not imagine you would prefer it thus, though I am clearly the last man to really know your preferences."

She abandoned any pretence of sewing. "I regret refusing you," she said quietly.

"I do not," he said. "For it taught me to be better than I could have been without having experienced that evening in the Hunsford parsonage. I had grown too used to thinking I could have anything I wanted, even people. I had become proud and conceited, but I hope that...I hope that now I am not.

"I *was* too proud, however, to go back to the carriage makers and tell them of my stupidity. So they have carried on. I had commissioned it with your pleasure in mind, and if Fitzwilliam was the one to have the privilege of giving it to you, then so be it. At least you would have had it."

"I have been so cruel to you, so harsh in my condemnations even until yesterday" she said, her eyes fixed on the material spread over the table and her lap. "I should have imagined you would like to take the carriage and run me over with it. Or, at the very least, tell the colonel he was welcome to me."

His hand came towards her, lingering over her arm for a moment before touching her gently. "I would not expect you to fully believe that I had changed on the strength of a few parties," he said. "And I know it must have been upsetting for you to learn about the wagers. I shall say to you though, in full honesty—a wager might have induced me to come here, but it would not make me pretend to feelings that were not my own. I love you. I did when I declared myself in Kent, and I do now. Wagers have nothing to do with it."

He hid nothing from her. When she managed to peep up at him again, she saw his feelings, naked and raw, plain in his eyes.

And that was when she heard the faint 'plunk' of a latch falling into place.

CHAPTER EIGHTEEN

"I might not be going to Brighton," Lydia told her sister, "but I am not going to lose all that allowance. If I must tell Papa myself that she kissed him, so I shall."

"What would Papa do about that?" Kitty asked with a little shake of her head. "Lizzy could tell him how you have kissed almost all of the officers."

"Have not!" Lydia retorted staunchly.

"Lizzy caught you kissing Denny," Kitty reminded her. "And I think she knows about that night we all played blind man's bluff."

Lydia's only reply to that was a slight huff of breath. It was a concern though; if Lizzy was made to marry for a mere kiss, then so too would be her sisters. She crossed her arms over her chest. "Very well then. We need more than a kiss in a maze."

"I do not even see Mr Darcy anywhere," Kitty said, looking over the room.

"Nor Lizzy. I saw her dance the first with Philips, but I have not the least notion what became of her after that."

"Oh, I know where she went."

"What?" Lydia grabbed her sister's arm. "Where is she?"

"I do not know precisely," Kitty said, wrenching her arm free. "But she planned to do some sewing below stairs."

"Sewing below stairs?" Lydia gaped at her. "What? Why?"

"I was listening to them talk this morning in their bedchamber. Jane hates her wedding gown, so she is going to wear Lizzy's gown and Lizzy will wear the one she hates. But it needed some alteration first. So she is below stairs tonight, taking care of that."

"Let us go and see if we can find her," Lydia decided. "And then we shall see what we can do to win this bet."

The Bennet girls knew Netherfield very well. The family who had once owned it, the Darlingtons, had had children much of an age with the Bennet girls, and many a happy day was spent playing games in its halls and begging cakes from its kitchen. Lydia, therefore, knew exactly where to go, and she and Kitty were there within minutes. They were not quite at the door when they heard the rumble of a male voice from within the small room that had once been a larder. Lydia gasped and grabbed her sister again, making her stop in her tracks.

"They are in there together," she mouthed to Kitty. Kitty replied by shoving her fist against her mouth as if to suppress giggles.

It took Lydia only seconds to decide what to do.

Motioning to Kitty to stay where she was, she tiptoed over to the door and engaged the latch.

"Run!" she mouthed silently at her sister, and so the two flew silently down the hall and up the stairs. When they reached the top again, the sound of their voices safely subsumed into the music, both girls burst out laughing. "If she stays in there with him long enough," Lydia said with a final hiccupping giggle, "she will have to marry him!"

"Let us go tell Papa we do not know where she is and that we are worried about her," Kitty said with a delighted giggle.

∽

"Did you hear that?" Elizabeth asked.

"It sounded like someone latched the door." Mr Darcy went to it, attempting to open it.

"Perhaps it is merely stuck?"

He applied his shoulder to the door, to no effect. Then he turned slowly and met her gaze. "It seems we are locked in."

"Mrs Nicholls or one of the footmen must have come by and done it, not realising I was still in here," she said.

He turned back to the door, pounding it with the flat of his hand. "Halloo! Is anyone out there?" He repeated it several times more, but not a sound was heard without.

"Save your voice, sir," Elizabeth said at last. "And your hand. I do not hear anyone out there. Someone must be...playing a trick, perhaps." She believed she had heard a giggle, quick and instantly muffled, right after the sound of the latch. *Probably Lydia,* she thought, *exacting her revenge.*

Mr Darcy nodded and ran his hand across his mouth, a gesture that he did, Elizabeth had noticed, when he was thinking. He came back to where she still sat and took his chair again. "We may be trapped in here for some time," he said gravely.

She nodded.

"Will your mother miss you?"

"I am not certain. At some point later in the evening, Jane was meant to make an excuse for me to return home —so that I might sew her gown without my mother knowing. And you?"

He grimaced and shook his head. "Likely the first I would be missed would be by my man, much later tonight."

"We are well and truly trapped, perhaps all night." She chuckled weakly, but it turned into a sigh. "So much for my good reputation."

"Obviously I would..." He frowned, shaking his head, and uttered a little groan. "I want so much to marry you, but the last thing I wish for is your father to force you to accept me."

"Then perhaps we ought to get ahead of him." The words just came out of her, with no forethought whatso-ever, but as soon as she said them, she knew it was right. Her boldness made her flush, even as elation made her heady and weak-kneed.

"Get ahead of him?"

Her mouth had gone very dry. There was too much within her to know how to say what she wished to say;

indeed, she was only just beginning to know it herself. She took a breath, then another as the first did not seem to perform its office. "If we were engaged first, then my father would have no cause to do anything, except maybe scold me a little."

He stared at her. "What do you mean?"

She laughed and looked away, suddenly shy. "I mean...you know what I mean."

"Do you mean that, perhaps, if you were forced to marry me, it would not be too much of a punishment?"

"I mean that I do not require forcing. The only thing which forces me to marry you is...is the leanings of my own heart."

He extended one arm, so she put aside the gown and the needle and the thread and reached her hand to join his. He used it to pull her towards him, and she found herself nestled against his chest, halfway onto his lap.

She could hear the rapid pounding of his heart, and it made her soft inside, thinking that she had caused it to do that. "What I mean to say," she said softly, "is that I have fallen in love with you."

He took her face in one hand, holding her tight with the other, and kissed her deeply. It surprised her, and thrilled her, and took her breath away, particularly when he punctuated his kisses with words of love and devotion, spoken against her mouth and cheek.

She hardly knew how long it was until they stopped kissing and resumed speaking. He wished to know how it was that her feelings for him had changed.

"Do you remember at Hunsford Parsonage when you

said that you liked me against your will, your reason, and your character?"

"I said many foolish things that night."

"No, but I have at last understood you! You meant to say that sometimes the person who seems to suit us the least is the very person who in talent and disposition is most perfect for us." She smiled. "And that person, for me, is you. You may be quiet while I am lively, and serious when I am gay—"

"I have long understood that your liveliness is just what I need to perhaps soften my own severity, and improve my manners. And I have hoped that there are things within my own nature that could add to your character as well."

"Your superior understanding of the world," she supplied. "And your excellent judgment. I have long known I could not marry a man that I did not respect as my superior—Mr Collins taught me that immediately— and even when you angered me, I still had to respect you for your honour and your probity, among other things."

He was vastly pleased she had said so; she could read it in his face. "You have said more than I might ever have dreamt of on entering this room." He glanced around. "This delightful, charming room that I shall forever honour. But I must say one more thing to you, and that is simply that I love you, dearly and completely, and will make it always my foremost object to see that you are happy."

"I love you too," she said. "And it will be my glad delight to see to your happiness for all of my days."

~

"You locked them in?" Wickham asked Miss Lydia.

He had not been invited to the ball—likely Darcy had seen to *that*—but Miss Lydia had urged him to come regardless, saying that so long as he arrived late enough to miss the reception line, no one would notice him among the officers. He had to, after all, to see how Darcy was doing. He had determined that, if need be, he would do as he must to ensure Darcy got the girl, so that he would get his money.

But it seemed dear Miss Lydia had taken care of things in his stead.

"I did!" she replied unrepentantly. "They fight all the time. They will either kill one another or end up in love, I am sure of it."

Wickham wondered when it was that Miss Lydia had become so perspicacious. "Well, let us go see how things are proceeding."

Very shortly thereafter, they were tiptoeing down the hall below stairs, by the kitchen. They both listened for a time, hearing nothing at all coming from within. Wickham had just turned to ask Miss Lydia whether she was certain they were yet in there when he heard it—a little breathy moan of pleasure.

Miss Lydia's eyes flew wide, and she looked like she might burst out laughing, so Wickham grabbed her by the hand and they ran, silently, a short distance away where they could speak without fear of being heard. As soon as she could, Miss Lydia burst into giggles.

Wickham barely stopped himself from kissing her.

Vexatious as she was, she had singlehandedly won the bet for him. He knew not to what extent the pot had grown, but reckoned he was in for a sizeable piece. Would Hurst, he wondered, know the fullness of it? Or could he be perhaps contented with some part of what he was owed so that Wickham himself might enjoy the rest?

"Lizzy must have accepted him. She would never be so wanton otherwise," Miss Lydia said with another burst of giggles.

"So it seems she has," Wickham agreed. Elizabeth Bennet had always seemed to be the fiery sort, Wickham thought ruefully, and Darcy had so long denied himself carnal pleasure, he would be a powder keg to her flame. Who knew what some time in supposed privacy might result in for the pair of them?

"Let us give them about half an hour more. Then you will go to your father and tell him you are worried about your sister. Send him down here to catch them—that should lead to some fun, to be sure!"

"There was something I wondered about," Elizabeth said.

For a man presently incarcerated in a cupboard, Darcy was blissfully happy. He should be well pleased to remain a week if it meant he was with her. *Though I doubt I could remain a gentleman for a week*, he thought. *It will be hard enough if we must stay here until Mrs Nicholls retires for the night.*

"What is that?"

"I thought it very strange—did not you?—that your

cousin should have been given land and yet seemingly had no interest in going to see it."

"That is true," he said slowly. "I should have imagined he would be travelling to Salt Hill straightaway."

"Salt Hill? He told me it was called Saint's Hill! And I thought it doubly strange when he told me that he had never seen the place despite it being quite close to Matlock and the seat of his own relation. Surely at some point he would have seen the place?"

"No, it is not in Derbyshire. Middlesex, I believe."

"He told me Derbyshire. I am certain of it."

There *was* something amiss in it all; Darcy could not quite put his finger on it. He had been so very occupied with winning Elizabeth that he had paid no mind to Fitzwilliam and his new land. It was difficult to make himself care about it, however, not with Elizabeth on his lap, absently winding her fingers in the curls at his neck.

"Do you think it is possible..." Elizabeth began slowly. She stopped herself then, saying, "No, that cannot be."

"What cannot be?"

"Lord Saye accidentally said something to me yesterday. He started to say 'that is why we—' but then he stopped himself and would say no more, save for one other comment about the colonel's intentional cruelty to you—which his lordship described as needful."

"Needful?"

She nodded. "They were both, it seems, excessively alarmed by the notion of you proposing to Miss de Bourgh. To add to all of that, I began to think of how strangely the colonel has behaved towards me, almost as if he wished to give the appearance of wooing me, but not actually wooing me."

"No?"

"Not at all. Either that, or it was the most clumsy attempt to woo a woman that I have ever known." She smiled up at Darcy then and added, "Bar none."

He had to just give her one more little kiss for that.

She then added, "I think it might have been made up."

It took Darcy a moment to understand her. "You think they... No. It is too devious, even for them."

"I do not think there was ever any estate, nor any real wish for the colonel to court or marry me. I think it might have been some scheme to prevent you from proposing to Miss de Bourgh. I simply could not grasp that your own cousin, dear friend that he seemed to be to you, would have conspired to steal me from you, and right in front of you, no less."

Darcy examined the idea. Fitzwilliam had heard much of what happened that wretched night in Hunsford Parsonage. He had listened to Darcy rail against himself, the world, women in general, and the stupidity of society. Then he had told him he needed to get his bollocks out of his reticule, and go and win the lady. Darcy had refused. Then Fitzwilliam had sent Saye in to tell him the same thing. Saye had told him to pull his head out of his arse, and go woo the lady. Darcy had refused.

They had played billiards with the object being that if Darcy lost, he had to go to Hertfordshire and try again with his lady. Darcy won, and told them to bugger off. His cousins had cajoled, persuaded—even threatened him once or twice that if he did not go back to Hertfordshire, they would never speak to him again. He had ignored it all.

Until Fitzwilliam came in saying he would try to win her himself. Then, and only then, had Darcy been provoked into action. He cursed softly.

"He will never admit it," he told Elizabeth. "I do not doubt that you are correct, but we would never get him to tell us so."

Elizabeth smiled, a brilliant smile that provoked him to kiss her again. Amid receiving his kiss, she whispered, "It might be fun to call his bluff."

CHAPTER NINETEEN

"**W**hat is it exactly that you wish to show me?" Miss Goddard asked.

Saye had taken her below stairs, supposing he had done his duty to the party by dancing with his hostess and one or two other lady bumpkins. Now it was time to really make Miss Goddard see what she was missing, and perhaps get a kiss or two besides.

"Oh, I want to show you a lot of things," he said with a wicked grin. "And see lots of things from you in return."

"You, sir, are absolutely terrible."

"You would not wish for someone too sedate," he informed her as they strolled down a small hall. "I think I am just what you—"

The sound of pounding and a man calling out interrupted what he had been about to say. "That sounds like Mr Darcy," Miss Goddard said nervously. "Behind that latched door."

"So it does." Saye walked over to the door and

unlatched it while he called, "Darcy? Get the stallion back in the barn, man, I am opening the door."

Well, well, well, he thought as the door swung open. *Progress has certainly been made.* His eyes took note of his cousin's dishevelled hair and partly undone cravat and the slightest blush of whisker burn on Miss Elizabeth's lower face. *Nicely done, Darcy.*

"Saye, I insist on knowing something," Darcy said, looking surprisingly stern for a man whose breeches were certainly causing him significant discomfort. "How much a part of this farce were you?"

"Farce?" Saye did his best to appear innocent. "I am not sure I follow."

"I know that Fitzwilliam had no earnest intentions in pursuing Miss Elizabeth." Darcy crossed his arms over his chest. "Tell me the truth, Saye."

Briefly, Saye considered lying. Why give it up now?

"I cannot help but notice," said Miss Elizabeth, "that the colonel's new estate seems to undergo changes in name rather regularly. And if the truth must be told, his attempts at courting me were...lacklustre."

Blast! The clever sort of woman was Saye's least favourite, but she would do well for Darcy. After a few moments, he laughed. "It worked, did it not, Darcy? Here you are, happy in a closet with Miss Elizabeth rather than rotting in hell with Lady Catherine."

Darcy took a step towards him. "Saye—"

"See here, Darcy, I know you probably dislike the fun at your expense, but all's well that ends well, hm?"

"That is not what I intended to say. I can stand to be the object of a caper, but it does not follow that I shall not have my own share of the amusement as well. For now, we must conceal the fact that Miss Elizabeth and I are to marry."

Beside him, Miss Goddard exclaimed with a delight that mirrored Saye's own. Darcy had got his heart's wish and, from the pink of her cheeks and the look in her eyes, he surmised that Miss Elizabeth had as well.

"Keep it quiet? No can do, *mon ami.*" Saye gave the pair a regretful nod. "Too much money on the line."

"Ah yes, the money," said Darcy. "Cannot think the fellows who bet on Fitzwilliam will be eager to hear it was all a humbug."

"Devil take it!" Saye narrowed his eyes at his cousin. "You are not going to—"

"You may have my discretion," said Darcy, "as long as I have yours. I mean to have some amusement of my own now, at Fitzwilliam's expense."

Saye turned to Miss Elizabeth, who was looking at Darcy like he had just finished hanging the moon. "And you, madam? Do you mean to tell me you wish to be a party to some scheme at the expense of my brother?"

She directed her attention to him and smiled sweetly. "In fact, it was my idea."

In a short time, the sewing was sent back to Longbourn in the care of Darcy's coachman. Elizabeth encountered her father just as they had sent the man off. Any concerns he had for her whereabouts were easily dismissed with, "Locked in a room? Papa, you can clearly see I am not.

Mr Darcy has only been helping me arrange to get a package back to Longbourn. For the wedding."

"Oh, well, of course, if it is for the sake of the wedding, no effort is too much," Mr Bennet replied with a wry smile and a roll of his eyes. Then he nodded at Darcy, patted his daughter on the back, and ambled away in the direction of the card room.

"Now," said Elizabeth to Darcy. "Let us go find the colonel."

A set was reaching its completion just as they came into the room. The crowd was thick and gay, though the ragged edges of a good party had begun to show. Curls were falling out of coiffures, cravats were decidedly less snowy, and the matrons on the side had grown flushed and distracted-looking. Given the advantage of superior height, Darcy was quick to spot his cousin amid the dancers and gestured towards him to show Elizabeth as well.

Colonel Fitzwilliam had been dancing with one of Bingley's friends from London, a pretty girl whom Darcy identified as Lady Harriet Thorpe with a half-chuckle that Elizabeth did not fully comprehend. The colonel escorted his partner to her chaperon, and then came to join his cousin and Elizabeth. Lord Saye and Miss Goddard, with perfect timing, also emerged from the crowd to re-join them.

"And where, my dear girl, have you been hiding all evening?" Colonel Fitzwilliam asked her with mocking severity.

"The duties of a bridesmaid prevail over all else," she replied.

Miss Goddard tittered nervously, her eyes darting about as if she expected to be exposed somehow. Pranks were evidently not the usual course for her.

"Fitzwilliam," Darcy interjected in what sounded to Elizabeth like an exceedingly stern tone. "Miss Elizabeth and I need to speak to you."

With exaggerated good humour, the colonel pretended to grimace then hung his head. "I think I know what this may be about. Let us go into the hall."

He looked a little surprised that Miss Goddard and Lord Saye continued with them but said nothing about it. The hall was full of lingering people, so the viscount suggested moving onto the terrace that overlooked the maze. Elizabeth afforded it only the briefest glance before turning to Colonel Fitzwilliam, who spoke before she could.

"I suppose you would like to see me drawn and quartered." He leant over her with his exaggeratedly twinkly eyes while Elizabeth fought not to laugh.

"Because of the wagers?"

He nodded regretfully. "It all just went so far beyond our control, did it not, Darcy?"

Darcy, standing behind her, only made a small, noncommittal noise.

"I blame myself," said Lord Saye generously. "You know how fond I am of a good gamble."

"I *was* upset," she said to the colonel. "At first. I cannot deny that."

"I beg your forgiveness," he said quickly.

She waved that aside, putting a smile on her face. "But when I really thought about it, I came to understand the compliment of your affections, sir, and well…" She glanced at Darcy, then finished her sentence. "I accept."

The colonel also glanced at Darcy. "You accept? What do you mean?"

Elizabeth reached both of her hands to grasp both of his tightly. "We shall be so happy together at Stank Hill!"

The colonel tried to remove his hands, but she did not allow it, squeezing even more tightly and beaming at him even more delightedly. "Ah…yes," he said awkwardly. "I mean, Miss Elizabeth, I hope that—"

"Welcome to the family," Lord Saye said warmly while Miss Goddard beside him offered well-wishes albeit with an incongruous nervous giggle.

Elizabeth finally let go of the colonel's hands, and Darcy stepped forwards and clapped his cousin on the back. "If I had to lose, at least I lose her to a worthy gentleman like you, Fitzwilliam. I wish you both every happiness."

The colonel was beginning to get a panicky sort of look about the eyes and was darting glances all around him. "There…there are considerations…I mean…you do not truly wish to marry a soldier, Miss Elizabeth—do you?"

"But you will not be a soldier," Elizabeth said cheerfully. "A husband and landowner must tend his hearth!"

"I shall write to Father directly tomorrow," Lord Saye promised. "See if he cannot get things moving on the sale of your commission."

"The war cannot go on much longer," Mr Darcy added. "And Stink Hall needs you."

"I think an engagement might be a bit…hasty," the colonel said urgently. "And as much as I admire—"

"But the *wager*," Elizabeth pressed. "It was for an offer of marriage, yes?"

"Absolutely," Lord Saye added. "That was the wager, for Miss Elizabeth's hand in marriage."

The colonel gave him a slight frown. "I think there has been some…confusion—"

"And now you have won, just as you wished to," Elizabeth concluded brightly.

He was caught. Even in the darkness, one could see the colour of his complexion had darkened. He seemed not to know what to say next. Elizabeth looked over her shoulder at Darcy, thinking he should be the one to finish it off.

Darcy stepped close to his cousin and leant in, speaking in low tones into the colonel's ear. Elizabeth heard little of it but did hear a few words that caused her to raise her eyebrows. For such a proper gentleman, Darcy certainly was adept at knowing when to put propriety aside.

His words raised the colonel's eyebrows, too. Pulling away from his cousin, he said, "Faith, Darcy, do you kiss your sister with that mouth?"

Darcy smiled and looked very satisfied with himself. He stepped back and pulled Elizabeth against his side. "I shall tell you whom I do kiss with this mouth. My intended wife." And then he smiled down at Elizabeth and did just that.

CHAPTER TWENTY

"**W**hat is *this*?"

The screech could be heard, Elizabeth imagined, in St Albans. She had gone to her mother's room alone, dressed in the lace gown, in the hope of both lessening Mrs Bennet's shock and dampening her reaction to the change. "Mama, Jane decided she wished for a simpler gown and I—"

Mrs Bennet stood abruptly, and her maid, who had been halfway through dressing her hair, yelped as the curls fell out of her hands. "To marry in some sort of common-looking gown—"

"Is what Jane wants," Elizabeth finished firmly. "Mama, Bingley hates lace!"

Mrs Bennet observably thought about that. "No, he does not," she decided. "I have seen the lace on Miss Bingley's gowns, and I do not care what you think of her, she is a very elegant woman, always well dressed—"

"Yes, but Bingley does not choose her gowns, does

he? And he would hardly wish for his wife to look like his sisters, would he?"

Mrs Bennet opened her mouth to protest but then closed it again.

"And I hear that Mr Darcy quite likes lace," she continued. "A *lot* of lace."

In truth, Darcy had no opinion on lace, in abundance or not. He had not truly seen the problem with Jane's original gown but thought it a fine example of sisterly affection that Elizabeth had switched for her sister's happiness.

"We all know that Mr Darcy has no good opinion of you," Mrs Bennet retorted. As she said so, she sank back into her seat and gestured to the maid to continue with her hair. From that, Elizabeth thought the matter mostly settled.

"I have reason to think he might have changed his mind," she replied. "Who knows? If I wear a gown he thinks elegant…" She gave a little shrug and tried to look exaggeratedly hopeful.

"Oh, Lizzy." Mrs Bennet sighed. "It is so like you to need to follow in Jane's footsteps! I do not see that you can reasonably expect a man like Mr Darcy to have his head turned just because he sees you done up in a bit of extra lace. After all—if he was truly so fond of lace, he could have had Miss Bingley quite some time ago!"

That her mother would say such things had ceased to sting years ago, but it did not follow that it did not vex her. "That is true," Elizabeth conceded. "Nevertheless, I really do think I might have a chance. Perhaps enough of a chance to place a wager upon it?"

Mrs Bennet glanced at her in the mirror. "You want to bet me?"

"Not a real wager. Nothing of any significance," Elizabeth replied nonchalantly. "But what if I said that should I ever find myself engaged to Mr Darcy, I shall be permitted to have any small nothing of a wedding I should wish for."

"Small nothing of a wedding?" Mrs Bennet snorted. "My dear, you have no idea… Why, these people of the *ton* have five hundred people lined up outside St George's! Grand balls and dinners and all manner of celebration and—"

"Supposing I could secure him, then that would be the wedding I insist on. A wedding by licence, perhaps even in his house in town."

"And if I should win this wager, what do I get?" Mrs Bennet asked.

"If you win," Elizabeth said, "then whomsoever I marry, I shall marry in this gown, and you may plan things to your heart's content. We have our witness right here to confirm it."

She gave the maid a little wink, and the maid seemed to suppress a smile as she agreed.

~

When Darcy left Longbourn following Jane and Bingley's wedding breakfast, Mrs Bennet was no doubt quite certain she had won her wager with Elizabeth. She seemed less sure, however, when he reappeared two days later and asked to see Mr Bennet. He was shown into the master's study immediately while Mrs Bennet and her daughters straightened themselves and began sending eager but questioning looks around the room, save for Elizabeth who avoided any telling expressions.

"If it was Colonel Fitzwilliam," said Mrs Bennet, "I might have been more certain. He seemed to be paying her a bit more attention, but I put it down to her being one of the few from Hertfordshire that he was acquainted with."

Elizabeth who had just then risen to quit the room, smiled to herself at that. "As it is," she told her mother, "the colonel was quite taken with Lady Harriet Thorpe. Who knows how many weddings might spring forth from Jane's?"

She entered her father's study moments later to see him regarding Darcy somewhat dubiously. "Do not look like that, Papa," she said as she took the seat that Darcy helped her into and accepted his hand around her own. "I have already told you that Mr Darcy and I have found we were much more in accord than ever we suspected."

She was grateful she had spoken to her father privately on the subject the day prior. Phrases such as 'have you gone mad' and 'thought you hated him' would not have been well met in the present circumstance. Mr Bennet was nevertheless somewhat disgruntled and unhappy-looking as Darcy explained to him how much in love he was.

Darcy's declarations were undoubtedly no little source of astonishment. To hear a man who was widely believed to be taciturn and disagreeable tell her father that she was a woman most worthy of being pleased, that he was in no way her equal but would spend the rest of his days trying to make her happy, that he would every day and in every way feel his good fortune in having her—it was almost too much to bear in its sweetness.

About halfway through these expressions, Mr Bennet appeared to lose some of his churlishness and, indeed, almost smiled when Mr Darcy concluded by saying, "I can only assure you, sir, in the most violent of terms, that I love her more than I have ever loved anyone or anything. Many men say they are the happiest of men when a woman they love accepts their offer, but I truly mean it."

"And you, Miss Lizzy?" Mr Bennet asked. "Can you give me any such guarantees?"

"I can," she said softly. "I promise you, Papa, I do not wish to marry to be like Jane, or to become the wife of a great man. I have no thought for wealth or position or any such trivial thing. I have accepted Mr Darcy because I love him and, in truth..." She turned to look at her intended and concluded, "I find the idea of living without him quite insupportable."

Darcy did not exactly smile when she said that, but his countenance warmed and softened, and she had no doubt that her words meant a great deal to him.

"Well then." Mr Bennet cleared his throat. "I suppose this means more lace and finery is in order."

"There will be very little lace or finery needed at all," said Darcy.

They finished each other's sentences as they explained their plans. A licence would be obtained and, as the Season would be soon at its completion, most of

Darcy's acquaintance would be leaving town for their country seats.

"And therefore," Elizabeth concluded, "any excess of balls or parties would be undesirable."

"A small breakfast for family," Darcy added. "And following that, a wedding trip. After that, with your permission, Elizabeth would like to have her younger sisters come to Pemberley for the autumn."

"All of them?"

Elizabeth nodded.

Finally, Mr Bennet smiled genuinely. "You have my blessing."

EPILOGUE

One year later

To make the time of travail pass more quickly, Jane had recommended revisiting, in her mind, all the dearest moments from her first year of marriage. Thus Elizabeth—enormously round, exceedingly sweaty, and with white-hot pain twisting its way up into her abdomen—was attempting to do just that.

Their wedding had been as quiet an event as could be possible when one was related to anyone called Bennet. They married in London. Elizabeth wore a gown that was beautiful, and Darcy had looked so handsome it had taken her breath away. That had never really happened before, that particular lovestruck breathlessness, but it was a real condition, and it struck her hard, so much so that she had scarcely been able to speak her vows.

A deal had been struck between Darcy and his cousins after Bingley's wedding. He would not reveal to the rest of the men involved that the wager had been mostly farcical. Those who had bet on Fitzwilliam would be rightly outraged if they found out they had been deceived in the colonel's intentions, and his honour might have been seriously questioned. To avoid all such unpleasantness, Darcy insisted on half of the winnings. Saye grumbled a bit about that, but as he had made significant progress in courting Miss Goddard by then, he had grown inattentive to most anything else.

It did surprise Darcy to find that George Wickham, of all people, had wagered in his favour, but as Wickham took his winnings and went elsewhere, he did not think on it overmuch.

Darcy then promptly turned over the money—first in small but then in increasingly larger amounts—to Elizabeth's cousin Philips, to help him set up his business in town. Philips took the sums given and, although sometimes he lost a little, more often than not he gained, often quite substantially. Before a twelvemonth had passed, the name of her cousin's small firm was on everyone's lips, and they were beginning to have to turn away would-be investors—though Darcy asked for preference to be given to anyone who had lost money on the infamous wager. It was his own quiet way of redressing any unfairness or wrong against them.

Elizabeth had been deeply touched by his actions. He was a far more generous, more kindly man than she ever might have believed, to Philips as well as to her Gardiner relations. He had even remarked once—a bit indelicately —how different was Mr Gardiner from Mrs Bennet and Mrs Philips. Elizabeth had known exactly what he meant and not been offended.

After another time of agony, Elizabeth's thoughts drifted to her husband's family. She had expected a group of people similar to Lady Catherine de Bourgh. While that lady's brother, the Earl of Matlock, had much resembled her, his temperament was much more jovial. He was a man aware of his position but, like Lord Saye, determined to enjoy it to the fullest extent possible.

"You see how it is, Elizabeth," Saye had informed her at her first dinner with the family, when she had been married only a month. "They dance to my tune."

Elizabeth had replied by peering round the table. "They all seem to be sitting to me."

Saye had tutted. "Metaphor, madam. Charming things —they might have even heard of them in Hertfordshire. But my point remains. What Saye says goes, both at Matlock and beyond...and I have decided to like you."

It had made her laugh even if she had been somewhat irritated with him that night. She had overheard him speaking to his brother in the drawing room not half an hour earlier. He had said that Darcy was 'a filthy animal' and would 'have her increasing within the fortnight'. Fitzwilliam had said he thought she was likely with child already. Saye argued that no, Darcy would have done as he needed to prevent things, so as to have longer to enjoy her to himself. They were on the point of laying wagers when they caught sight of her and immediately walked off in different directions.

One year on, her marriage was far better than she ever might have imagined on that autumn night in Meryton, back in '11. Darcy was an attentive and loving husband— even now she could hear him outside the birthing room door, demanding that someone see to her comfort, someone make his baby come—and, as it turned out, one of the best men she knew. Nay—*the* best man she knew, bar none.

She continued in this way, her mind drifting around the happy scenes of the past twelvemonth, while her body was torn into shreds by the baby, until at last, just when it seemed she could bear no more, *he* was there.

"Lizzy!" Jane cried. "Oh, Lizzy, he is just lovely!"

Elizabeth felt benumbed both inside and out. Her legs and arms hardly even felt like her own as they were pushed and prodded back into some semblance of dignity on the bed. Her baby boy was swaddled in his blanket and placed within her arms. Jane was sent off to give the good news to the waiting men, who were there to calm Darcy and—Elizabeth suspected—collect bets on the gender of the child. Minutes later, pounding footsteps were heard and the door thrust open. The midwife, who had attended her throughout, startled and nearly dropped the basin she was holding.

Darcy looked boyish himself, his clothing rumpled and his hair disordered, likely from running his fingers through it. "Is this my son?" he asked, reverently approaching her bedside.

"Would you like to hold him?" Elizabeth's voice emerged weak and a bit croaky.

Darcy said not a word as he bent over and gently removed their child from her arms, then seated himself gingerly beside her. "He is perfect," he said, looking down at the wrinkled, red face. "Absolutely the most perfect child that ever was."

"Did you win?" she asked with as much of an impertinent smile as she could muster.

"Win?" He feigned confusion. "What do you mean, win?"

She gave him a disgusted look. "Disguise does not suit you, Mr Darcy, and we have an impressible child with us."

His eyes were soft when he looked at her. "Yes, I won. I won that autumn when I came into Hertfordshire and met a woman who taught me to be a better version of myself than I ever could have been without her. And I won when that woman permitted me a second chance to court her properly and when she accepted my offer of marriage. And I have won every single day since then, when I wake in the morning and see that no, this blessed life is not a dream but a reality." He leant over, still being cautious, and kissed her lips. "I love you."

His words made Elizabeth's heart warm, and she, rather needlessly, adjusted the baby's blanket. "I love you too—so very much," she murmured. Then with another smile, she said, "But pretty words aside—did you win the wager?"

"Thankfully, yes," he admitted with a chuckle. "Because I really would not have wanted to name our daughter after Saye."

The End

ABOUT THE AUTHOR

Amy D'Orazio is a longtime devotee of Jane Austen and fiction related to her characters. She began writing her own little stories to amuse herself during hours spent at sports practices and the like and soon discovered a passion for it. By far, however, the thing she loves most is the connections she has made with readers and other writers of Austenesque fiction.

Amy currently lives in Myrtle Beach with her husband and daughters, as well as three Jack Russell terriers who often make appearances (in a human form) in her books.

For the latest information on new releases and sales please follow Amy on Bookbub or her Amazon Author Page.

ALSO BY AMY D'ORAZIO

NOVELS

A Match Made at Matlock

A Lady's Reputation

A Short Period of Exquisite Felicity

A Wilful Misunderstanding

So Material a Change

The Best Part of Love

The Mysteries of Pemberley

∼

NOVELLAS

A Fine Joke

Heart Enough

Of a Sunday Evening

The Happiest Couple in the World

∼

SHORT STORY ANTHOLOGIES

An Inducement into Matrimony

Dangerous to Know: Jane Austen's Rakes & Gentlemen
Rogues (The Quill Collective)

Elizabeth: Obstinate Headstrong Girl (The Quill Collective)

Happily Ever After with Mr Darcy

Rational Creatures: Stirrings of Feminism in the Hearts of Jane Austen's Fine Ladies (The Quill Collective)

Yuletide: A Jane Austen-Inspired Collection of Stories (The Quill Collective)